CURSE OF THE BOGGIN

The Library ● Book 1

Also by D. J. MacHale

Voyagers: Project Alpha
The SYLO Chronicles
Morpheus Road series
Pendragon series

CURSE OF THE BOGGIN

The Library • Book 1

D. J. MacHale

Random House 🏠 New York

Text copyright © 2016 by D. J. MacHale
Jacket art copyright © 2016 by Shane Rebenschied
Jacket key and keyhole art copyright © 2016 by Leah Palmer Preiss

All rights reserved. Published in the United States by Random House Children's Books,
a division of Penguin Random House LLC, New York.

Random House and the colophon are registered trademarks of
Penguin Random House LLC.

Visit us on the Web! randomhousekids.com

Educators and librarians, for a variety of teaching tools, visit us at
RHTeachersLibrarians.com

Library of Congress Cataloging-in-Publication Data is available upon request.
ISBN 978-1-101-93253-7 (trade) — ISBN 978-1-101-93254-4 (lib. bdg.) —
ISBN 978-1-101-93255-1 (ebook)

Printed in the United States of America
10 9 8 7 6 5 4 3 2 1
First Edition

To all of my good buddies from Villanova

"Nothin's real scary except in books."

—JEAN LOUISE "SCOUT" FINCH IN *TO KILL A MOCKINGBIRD*

FOREWORD

Welcome, my friends.

We're about to begin a new adventure together. This is always a fun time for me because I know exactly what's in store for you, and you have *no idea* of what's coming. Mwahahahaha! Once you've read *The Curse of the Boggin,* you'll have a pretty good sense of what to expect from future books in The Library series. But as of right now it's a clean page, a blank slate, an empty screen.

A mystery.

If you've read my books, you know I like mysteries. Whether they're fantasy, science fiction, or thrillers, I like to keep you guessing. And, oh yes—I like spooky.

The Library is spooky.

I'm not sure why I often write about supernatural doings. I suppose you could ask my therapist. But seeing as I don't have a therapist, don't bother trying.

If I were to analyze it myself, I'd have to say it's because I like possibilities. When authors write stories about situations where the rules of science and nature don't necessarily apply, it creates a slew of opportunities to concoct imaginative scenarios and crazy challenges for characters to deal with. I guess that's the villain in me coming out. I like to make my characters sweat a little.

And my readers too.

Speaking of possibilities, The Library is going to be a bit different from my other series. If you've read Pendragon or Morpheus Road or The SYLO Chronicles, you know that all those stories build toward a conclusion. Whether it's one of three volumes or ten, each book is the next chapter in a grand overall story that has a definitive climax. Not so with The Library. Once you've read the first book (the one you're holding, duh), you can read the rest in any order. Each will hold a unique tale that doesn't necessarily rely on any of the others. (Except for the first. It's the setup. You've gotta start with number one. I said that, right?) There will be a continuing cast of characters you'll get to know, but they will find themselves in entirely different situations and confronted by uniquely weird dilemmas every time.

My plan is to explore all sorts of supernatural puzzles. The common thread will be the characters you are about to meet. They'll be going along on these adventures with you. And, believe me, I'm going to make them sweat. A lot. It's what I do.

Before you open the door to these odd archives, I'd like to offer some thanks to the people who helped bring this book to you.

Michelle Nagler, my editor at Random House Children's Books, was the first who dared to enter The Library. Michelle, Mallory Loehr, and Diane Landolf have thoughtfully guided its creation. To them and to all the good folks at RHCB, I thank you.

My support teams headed by Richard Curtis and Peter Nelson have had my back since *The Merchant of Death*. (And with Peter, since *Are You Afraid of the Dark?*) As always, thanks for taking care of business.

The solid encouragement and support of my wife, Evangeline, is, as always, invaluable, while the merciless criticism from my daughter, Keaton, is, as always, totally annoying. But it's also spot-on accurate. It's a double-edged sword there. Heck, Keaton wasn't even *born* until after *The Never War* was published. How can it be possible that she is able to figure out my plot twists? Smart kid, I guess. Or *my* kid. I love you both.

I am truly grateful to the hundreds of booksellers, librarians, and teachers I've had the good fortune to meet over the years. Whether you represent a big-box store, local indie, school, or massive district, you do such a wonderful job of promoting literacy by getting books into the hands of kids. Thank you.

And, of course, the biggest thanks must go to you, dear reader. One of the wonderful perks of writing my books for young people is that every year there are new readers who discover them, as well as loyal readers who have been with me for years. It's great to hear, "I grew up with your stories!" Though it does make me feel kind of ancient. But that's okay; it's worth it. Sort of. Seriously, I can't tell you how much I enjoy hearing from you all so that I can answer your questions and discuss the stories . . . even if you enjoyed them way back when you were a kid.

Okay now. Back to the main reason we're here.

This series is about books. Scary books. If you're reading this foreword, it means I'm speaking your language. You're just as interested in dark mysteries as I am, aren't you? Well, my friend, you've come to the right place. Settle in. Get comfortable. We're setting out on a journey together. It's one of those trips where you won't be quite sure what you're going to find behind the next closed door or what you'll run into when you round a corner. Things won't always be what they seem. Did that shadow move, or was it a trick of the flickering light? Who can I trust? Who should I fear?

Am I going to be able to get to sleep tonight?

No promises about that last one.

It's all there waiting for you. So let's turn the page, open the door, and step into . . .

The Library.

—D. J. MacHale, 2016

Prologue

It was under the bed.

Parents always tell their children there's nothing scary down there, or lurking in the deep depths of a closet, or hiding low in dark shadows. That's what parents always say, and they're right.

Most of the time.

Alec Swenor had something under his bed that night, and it wasn't dust bunnies.

"Again?" his mother, Lillian, asked with frustration. "I've checked under there every night for a week, and I always find the same nothing."

"I'm sorry," Alec complained. "It's not my fault I keep hearing things."

Alec's bedroom was a typical nine-year-old's room. The

walls were covered with *Avengers* posters, a small desk had a computer that was mostly used to play *Minecraft,* and a long shelf held a vast collection of his favorite books.

He watched nervously from a safe distance as his mother knelt down next to the bed to examine the dark below. Mrs. Swenor got down low so that her face was barely inches from the floor. She lifted the Jedi bedspread, peered underneath, and . . .

"Ahhh!"

Alec jumped back with surprise. "I told you!"

"I don't believe it!" his mother exclaimed as she reached under the bed and pulled out a plate of day-old scrambled eggs.

She held out the congealed mess as if it were diseased. "You told me you finished your breakfast," she said, annoyed.

Alec let out a relieved breath. "I ran out of time. It was either eat breakfast or tie my shoes."

"Or you could have gotten out of bed ten minutes earlier."

"I'm sorry. I was tired. I haven't been sleeping so hot."

Mrs. Swenor softened. "I know, sweetheart. But please believe me, there's no boogeyman down there."

She kissed Alec on top of his head and walked toward the bedroom door. "I love you, even if you are a nutjob."

She left with the plate of stinky eggs, passing her husband, Michael, who was watching the scene from the door, looking more worried about the situation than his wife was.

"You okay, bud?" he asked his son with genuine concern.

"Yeah," Alec replied, embarrassed.

"Want to sleep with us tonight?"

"Nah, I'm being dumb."

"No, you're not. You know you can always shout, and we'll come running. No matter what. Okay?"

"Okay, Dad."

"Good night. I love you."

"I love you too."

Michael Swenor gave a last, concerned look to his son, then left, gently closing the door behind him.

Alec gazed across the room to his bed. It was as normal as any bed on the face of the planet. He had absolutely no problem with it.

Until a few days ago.

It began with subtle scratching, as if rats were scurrying below. The Swenors' apartment was on the top floor of an old four-story brownstone in New York City. It wouldn't be weird for rats to be scampering under the floorboards.

Then came the knocking.

Rats didn't knock.

Alec would run out of the room and drag his parents back in to listen, but each time, the sounds had stopped before his mom and dad arrived. During the day, Alec felt silly for being so scared. But at night, when all was quiet, things were different.

Alec sprinted across the floor and flung himself the last few feet into the bed in case blood-soaked claws were waiting to reach out and grab his ankles. He dug under the covers, lifted them up to his chin, and listened.

Nothing.

All he heard was the far-off wail of a police siren and the white noise of the city beyond his closed window. He believed his mom. There was no boogeyman under his bed. It was silly to act like a jumpy two-year-old instead of a mature nine-year-old. He scrunched his eyes shut, and after a long twenty minutes, he fell asleep without having heard any more weird sounds.

All was well.

Until just after midnight.

There's no logical reason why strange doings begin when the day changes, but that's often how it goes.

The scratching returned.

Alec's eyes snapped open as though he had heard the crash of a cymbal. He lay very still. Whatever was under his bed was back. His panic grew and his mouth went dry. He wanted to yell for his parents, but his throat was closed so tight, he couldn't utter a peep.

Then came the knocking. Whatever was down there was alive. Or at least alive enough to be making sounds. He couldn't take it anymore. He had to know what it was.

Slowly, moving his body as if it weighed a ton, he peered over the edge of the bed, toward the floor.

His Jedi blanket was half off the bed and bunched below. Moonlight streamed in through the window, providing enough light for Alec to make out the image of Chewbacca with his head thrown back midroar. All was normal.

Until the blanket moved.

Oddly, it didn't scare him. Instead, it confirmed that something was really there. Something normal. Something real. Nothing spooky. It was probably a rat. Alec hated rats, but they didn't scare him. Enough! He reached down and yanked the blanket back.

What he saw was something far stranger than a common rat.

Words were scratched into the floorboards. Words that hadn't been there before. They looked to have been crudely scraped by a knife.

Or a claw.

Alec had to lean down close to read them.

"'Surrender the key,'" he read aloud.

He reached for the floor, wanting to touch the etched letters to figure out if they were real or a trick of light. His hand slowly dropped lower, growing closer to the mysterious message. As his fingertips were about to touch the odd markings, an ominous growl came from under the bed.

Rats didn't growl.

Alec pulled his hand back quickly and cowered against the wall as . . .

. . . the Jedi blanket came to life. It flew across the floor to the center of the room, stopped suddenly, and fell to the floor, revealing the culprit.

It was a dog. A pit bull. Its head was nearly as large as its muscular body, with jaws that split its skull, like a leering jack-o'-lantern . . . with teeth. Fangs, actually. The beast turned to face Alec and tensed, staring him straight in the eye.

This was not a friendly dog.

"Dad!" Alec called out weakly, fearing his words might trigger the beast.

The animal stood between him and the door, its body as tense and tight as a banjo string, staring at Alec.

Alec glanced toward the window above his bed. It was his only option. He lunged for it, threw it open, and rolled out onto the metal landing of the fire escape.

Behind him, the dog sprang.

"Dad!" Alec finally shouted out.

He slammed the window shut as the powerful animal launched. It drilled the glass with its head, creating a spider-web of cracks. The window didn't shatter, but that didn't stop the beast. It hammered away at the glass, butting with its head again and again, determined to break through.

Alec had to move. His family's apartment was on the top floor. Climbing up to the roof would be fast and easy. He grabbed the metal rungs of the ladder and made the short climb. He was only a few feet from the top when the window below him shattered and the dog blasted through in an explosion of broken glass.

Alec froze and looked down to see the animal staring up at him with angry red eyes.

"Leave me alone!" he screamed at the beast.

He threw himself over the low safety wall, onto the black, tar-papered surface, and ran for his life. It was the dead of night. The only light came from the city and the moon and stars above. He dashed to the far side of the roof, hoping there would be another fire escape. When he reached the edge of the building, he looked over to see . . . no fire escape. He spun around, frantically looking for a doorway that might lead back down to the fourth floor. What he saw instead was the pit bull standing on the far edge of the roof, staring back at him.

How did it climb the ladder? Alec thought.

He didn't have time to come up with an answer, because as soon as the dog locked eyes with Alec, it leapt off the safety wall and ran directly toward him.

Alec spun around, desperate to find an escape route. This time he saw something he hadn't noticed before. A

7

metal ladder was attached to the outside of the building. How could he have missed that? Didn't matter. It was his only hope.

The vicious dog was halfway to Alec and charging hard. Thick slobber flew from its mouth as it bared its sharp fangs. Alec had to move. He ran the few feet to the top of the metal ladder, threw his legs over the edge, and began to climb down as . . .

. . . the ladder disappeared. Vanished. *Poof.* Gone.

Alec had already committed to going over, and he fell. Desperately, he grabbed for the roof and managed to catch the edge. He hung there by the fingertips of both hands, his bare feet dangling four stories above the hard pavement. So many thoughts flashed through his head: *How could I have been so stupid? Why did I think there was a ladder? Will the dog bite my fingers?*

The dog.

Alec heard the scraping of its claws as it arrived at the edge of the roof. He looked up, expecting to see the dog looming over him, dripping slobber.

Instead, peering down at him was an old woman.

"Help me!" Alec called to her.

She had waist-length gray hair and wore a long forest-green dress. Over it was a black shawl that she clutched to her chest with a bone-white hand. The tendrils of hair blew about her head like a pack of wild dancing spirits. Though

8

her face was pale and wrinkled like that of someone a hundred years old, her eyes were focused and alive with fiery madness.

Alec's brief moment of relief was shattered when he looked into those horrible eyes.

"Dad!" he screamed in desperation.

He didn't have the strength to hang on much longer.

"Save me!" he cried to the woman. "Please!"

The woman leaned down over the edge to stare him straight in the eye.

"Oh no," she replied in a low, dark voice that sounded like the hollow echo from an empty grave. "That wouldn't help me at all. Now, if you don't mind ... please fall."

"Dad!" Alec screamed again ...

... and lost his grip.

His fingers slipped off the edge, and he began to fall as ...

... a hand shot down and grabbed his wrist, stopping him from a death plummet. He was quickly hauled up and over the edge as if he weighed no more than one of his Transformers toys. A second later he was deposited safely on the roof.

"Dad!" Alec cried, and threw his arms around his father.

"You're okay," Michael Swenor said soothingly as he hugged his son to his chest. "I promise."

"Where is she?" Alec asked, looking about with fear. "Where did she go?"

"Who?"

"The old lady. She wanted me to fall. And there was a dog under my bed. And a ladder, but it disappeared. I swear! I'm not lying!"

"I know you're not lying," Mr. Swenor said, his voice cracking with emotion as he fought back his own tears. "Let's get back to your mother, and we'll talk about it."

Alec reluctantly released his bear hold on his father.

"Do you know what happened, Dad?" he asked.

Michael Swenor took a deep breath before replying, as if the answer pained him.

"I do, and it's a long story," he finally said. "It's time you heard it. All of it. Your mom too."

"So you believe me?" Alec asked, finally getting control of himself.

"I do."

Michael Swenor stood up and reached his hand down to take his son's. "Let's go see Mommy."

They never connected.

The pit bull was back.

It came charging across the roof like a runaway freight train.

"Look out!" Alec screamed.

Michael Swenor barely had time to look up before the dog leapt at him. He instinctively backed away, but he was too close to the edge of the roof. He stumbled, hit the low safety wall, and tumbled over.

"No!" Alec screamed.

In the bedroom below, Lillian Swenor heard the scream. Her entire body tensed as if she had been hit with an electric prod. She was momentarily frozen, unsure of what she should do.

In her heart she knew there was nothing.

She looked around at Alec's room as if she might find an answer there. The window was open. It wasn't shattered; it was just open. Michael had opened it when they came running in after hearing Alec's frightened cries. There was no broken glass, no hint of the terror that had visited Alec and chased him onto the roof.

There was only one clue to the mystery that remained.

Mrs. Swenor looked down at the floor through tear-filled eyes, as if in a dream. She ran her fingers across the words that had been carved into the wood.

Surrender the key.

The words were still there.

"Oh, Michael," she whispered to no one. "What have you done?"

CHAPTER

1

"Use your brains, people, for a change," Mr. Winser commanded impatiently as he prowled the aisles of third-period social studies class, hunting for his next victim.

Winser had been teaching seventh-grade social studies since before I was born. Maybe before my parents were born. He was a fossil who wore wide ties that were so ugly, I couldn't tell if the hideous patterns were intentional or just a bunch of stains from spilled food.

"Can someone *please* offer me an intelligent response?" he asked with disdain. "What were some of the negative impacts of evolution between the *Homo erectus* period and the *Homo sapiens* period?"

Winser spun and pointed his finger at an unsuspecting girl.

"Miss Oliver!" he declared.

Gwen Oliver sat bolt upright, as if lightning had flown from Winser's fingertip. Gwen wasn't a social studies scholar. Or a math scholar. Or any kind of scholar, for that matter. She was the kind of girl who did her best to get through the day without having to think too much. Or at all.

"Umm . . . ," she said, stalling, hoping Winser would move on.

"Unacceptable!" he shouted. He said that a lot. "Stand up. Get the blood flowing to that underused brain of yours."

Gwen gave him an uncertain look and didn't budge.

"I said stand!" Winser barked.

She stood slowly, with her shoulders slumped, while tugging at her long auburn hair nervously. All eyes were fixed on her. If it wasn't her worst nightmare, it sure came close.

"Now, fill the room with your knowledge. Enlighten us all with your insightful thoughts on evolution."

He might as well have asked her to explain cold fusion.

"I . . . I don't know," she said in a voice so small that only highly trained rescue dogs could have heard it.

"Unacceptable," he barked. "Have you read the material?"

Gwen nodded and shrugged.

"What does that mean?" he said, making an exaggerated shrug, imitating her.

Gwen shrugged again. She looked ready to cry.

"I'll answer for you," he said. "You read it, but you didn't understand it. Would that be accurate?"

Gwen gave him a sad smile and a weak nod.

"Pathetic. Sit!" Winser commanded, as if talking to a dog. "These are not difficult concepts, except to you, maybe."

Gwen sat down, both relieved and humiliated. She may not have understood the chapter on evolution, but she sure didn't deserve to be treated like that.

Winser spun and pointed right at me.

"Marcus O'Mara."

I didn't flinch. I was hoping he'd nail me.

"I'm giving you a gift, Mr. O'Mara!" Winser exclaimed. "The underwhelming Miss Oliver is an easy act to follow." He chuckled at what he thought was a clever remark.

Nobody else did.

I stared straight at the guy and didn't answer.

"Well?" Winser said impatiently.

I looked him square in the eye and didn't say a word.

"Did you hear me, Mr. O'Mara? Or are your ears as disengaged as your brain?"

I did my best impersonation of a statue.

"Should I interpret your silence as proof that you don't understand the material either?"

I gave him nothing. Not a twitch. Not a blink.

Winser fidgeted nervously. He wasn't used to having kids do anything but tremble in fear when he got in their faces.

"I'm waiting for a response, Mr. O'Mara," Winser said, with a touch of uncertainty.

I stood up, slowly, and walked deliberately to the front of the class. I don't think anybody was breathing, because the only sounds I heard were those of my own footsteps. I walked to the whiteboard, picked up a marker, and in bold blue letters wrote:

YOU'RE A TEACHER. TRY TEACHING.

When I hit the period for emphasis, the class erupted in cheers.

Winser's face went red with rage. He raised his hands, and the class quieted down, waiting for the next move.

"That buys you two days' detention," he said through clenched teeth.

I turned back to the board and wrote:

AND YOU'LL STILL BE A LOUSY TEACHER.

The class broke out in wild applause and whistles.

I held the marker out toward Winser, stared him down, and dropped it to the floor.

Boom!

The kids all jumped to their feet and cheered. Even Gwen Oliver joined in, smiling broadly.

That afternoon, after school, I found myself in an empty classroom, spending the first of *five* days in detention. I didn't care. We're always getting lectures about the evils of bullying. In my opinion, those rules apply to teachers too.

To be honest, I didn't hate being in detention. It gave me a chance to do homework. Okay, it *forced* me to do homework. At least I'd be done and could watch some TV at home. Gotta look on the bright side.

"Seriously?" came a voice from outside. "You dropped the marker and did a walk-off?"

"You're out of your mind," came another voice.

Standing outside the open window were my two friends, Annabella Lu and Theo McLean.

Lu was hard to miss. She was Chinese American, with straight jet-black hair that was blunt-cut to just below her jaw, and bangs that barely cleared her eyes. While most girls wore subtle lip gloss, Lu's lips were always a shocking red. Her pale skin made them stand out even more, like a talking stoplight. She wore a red

16

plaid shirt over a black T-shirt and cutoff jeans. None of the other girls looked anything like Lu, which was exactly what Lu was going for.

I called her Lu because Annabella had way too many syllables.

"The guy is a tool," I said with a shrug.

"And now you're a legend," Lu said.

"I don't want to be a legend."

"Then be careful. People might start liking you."

"You've set a bad precedent," Theo said. "Now Winser will be gunning for you all year."

Theo always talked like a professor giving a lecture. He was a black guy who dressed as though he'd just come from brunch at some country club. His shirts and khakis were always ironed as smooth as paper. He wore ties too. Bow ties. Basically, he looked like the kind of guy who would get beaten up every day. The only reason he didn't was because he had an insurance policy.

Me.

Nobody messed with me.

"It's only October," Theo said. "There's a whole lot of seventh grade left."

"Yeah, for Winser too," I said. "If he doesn't lighten up, neither will I."

"I don't like it," Theo said with a deep frown. "This can only get worse."

"Five days of detention," Lu said. "Was it worth it?"

"What do *you* think?" I asked her.

"What do *I* think?" Lu asked with surprise. "Do you have to ask? Have we met? Yeah, it was worth it."

"Thank you," I said.

"Gotta go," Lu said. "I've got practice."

She pushed away and sped toward the sidewalk on roller skates. Lu was a roller-derby girl. *Lu-na-tic* was her derby name. Perfect. In a flash of plaid and long legs, she was gone.

"Do you need anything?" Theo asked.

"Jeez, Theo, relax. It's detention, not prison."

"All righty," he said.

Yes, Theo used the phrase *all righty* a lot. If he weren't my best friend, I'd probably want to beat him up myself.

"I'll see you tomorrow," he said, and headed off the other way.

I didn't have a lot of friends at Stony Brook Middle School. Okay, I had exactly two. Lu and Theo. I wasn't a group guy. The three of us didn't care about being on the "popular" track, which meant you had to wear the same clothes as everyone else and make fun of anyone who didn't conform. We did whatever we wanted because we didn't care what anybody else thought about us. It was total freedom.

I checked the clock. Twenty minutes left on day

number one of my sentence. Piece of cake. I pulled out my earth science textbook and was about to explore the wonders of magma when I got a strange feeling . . . as if I was being watched. I looked back to the window to see if Lu or Theo had come back.

They hadn't.

But I wasn't alone.

I looked toward the open door of the classroom and saw a man standing there, staring at me with a totally blank expression. As if that wasn't weird enough, he was wearing pajamas and a bathrobe.

It sent a cold shiver up my spine.

"You looking for somebody, chief?" I asked.

Crash! The sound of breaking glass came from outside in the hallway. It was so loud and so sudden, I actually jumped in my seat.

The guy in the doorway barely reacted. He looked down the hallway to my right, then turned and slowly walked away in the opposite direction.

I leapt up from the desk and ran to investigate. When I peered out the door, into the hall, I shouted after the guy, "Hey! What was that—?"

The guy was gone. Huh? He should have been a few feet away, but he was nowhere to be seen. I guessed he must have ducked into the next classroom. Odd.

I looked the other way and saw what had made the

crashing sound. Halfway down the hall, a glass trophy case was completely destroyed.

Whoa.

"Ms. Holden!?" I called out.

Holden was the assistant principal and my detention warden. She had stepped out of the classroom a while earlier to do whatever assistant principals do after school. Wherever she was, she didn't answer.

I walked the twenty yards to the damage, my sneakers crunching on broken glass as I got closer. The case had held years of trophies and plaques won by long-forgotten teams. The remnants were strewn everywhere. Some were broken in two, others totally mangled. The glass window that had protected it all (ha!) lay in a million tiny pieces on the floor. Whoever had done this wouldn't get away. The guy in his jammies must have seen it all happen.

I took a step closer and crunched glass again. I jumped back quickly and looked down to see something on the floor that was, in a word, impossible.

Tiny bits of glass were scattered everywhere, but directly beneath the case the debris was arranged into a pattern that spelled out words. Actual words, formed by thousands of small glass fragments, like a mosaic.

" 'Surrender the key,' " I read out loud.

My mind spun, trying to make sense of it. Could the glass have landed that way randomly? No way. But there hadn't been time for somebody to set it up.

Crash!

The vandal was still at work. The sound had come from around the corner at the end of the hallway. I sprinted toward it, reached the end of the hall, turned the corner, and saw the culprit.

My knees went weak.

Standing twenty yards in front of me was a massive black bull.

Yes, a bull.

"Holy . . ."

The animal swung its head from side to side in agitation, flashing its long, pointed horns. It was an eight-hundred-pound monster that looked more like shadow than substance.

I had no idea how to react until the bull fixed its eyes on me.

The animal stiffened, chuffed, and pounded a hoof on the floor. I had seen enough movies about bullfights to know this wasn't good. I didn't dare move for fear of pulling the trigger on the monster and releasing its fury.

On me.

"Mr. O'Mara?"

I shot a look to my left to see Ms. Holden standing beyond the classroom I'd just come from. Bad move. As soon as I broke eye contact, the bull charged.

There was only one thing to do.

Run.

"Move!" I shouted to Ms. Holden as I sprinted toward her.

Holden kept walking closer, looking confused.

"What are you doing?" she asked.

The bull reached the corner behind me, its hooves slashing at the linoleum to maintain traction, but it couldn't make the turn. It skidded and slammed into the far wall with a huge thud and a pained grunt. The floor shook with the force of impact, but, rather than slowing the beast down, the crash only fueled its rage. It let out a furious bellow that made the hairs go up on the back of my neck. I sprinted through the broken glass in front of the destroyed trophy case, crunching over the gritty surface, fearing I would slip and fall.

The bull was on the move again and closing in fast.

Ms. Holden continued walking toward me with her hands out and palms up in a "What is going on?" gesture.

"Get out of the way!" I screamed.

The bull let out a chilling howl. I had no idea bulls could howl. I was sure I could feel its hot breath on my neck. No way I could outrun this monster. In seconds I'd be trampled. Or gored. Or trampled and then gored.

"Get in the classroom!" I yelled.

I cut the angle and headed for the doorway.

The thundering sound of hooves on the hard floor grew louder. It was going to be close. I braced, ready to feel the points of the bull's horns stabbing me in the back. I hit the brakes and slid across the waxed floor. For a second I thought I'd overshoot the door, but my sneakers caught, and I threw myself into the room. I instantly hit a desk in the first row and tumbled to the floor in a tangle of books and furniture. I vaguely heard the sound of the enraged bull galloping past the open door like a freight train on its way to another station.

When I looked up to get my bearings, I saw that I wasn't alone.

The guy in the bathrobe was back. He stood with his arms at his sides, totally calm in spite of the pandemonium. He reached into the pocket of his bathrobe, took out a brown leather cord, and held it out to me. Hanging from it was a key. An oversized, old-fashioned brass key.

He held it out as if offering it to me.

I got to my knees, my eyes focused on the dangling key that swung in front of my face hypnotically. I reached out to grab it, but when I closed my fingers around the key, my hand passed through it as if it was nothing more than a projection. A shadow. An illusion.

A ghost.

I looked to the guy, questioning. He gave me a sad shrug.

"Mr. O'Mara!"

I spun back to see Ms. Holden standing in the doorway with her hands on her hips, looking totally peeved.

Reality had returned.

I jumped up and ran to her, stumbling over books and nearly tripping over the desk again.

"Are you okay?" I asked.

"Am I okay?" Holden replied angrily. "What in the world is wrong with you?"

"What do you think?" I said, incredulous. "The bull!"

"Yeah, that's a good word for it," Holden said with a frown. "Explain yourself."

My mind raced. Nothing was adding up. I ran past her to the door.

"What's to explain?" I exclaimed. "You saw it."

I peered out into the hallway to see . . . no bull. I looked to the smashed trophy case.

The glass was intact. The trophies were undamaged. There was no shattered glass, and there were no words written in glass fragments on the floor.

Huh?

I stood staring, trying to understand what I was seeing. Or not seeing.

Then I remembered.

"Ask him! He saw it!" I exclaimed, and spun around. "Hey, chief, tell her about the—"

The guy was gone.

"Wha—?" I sputtered as I scanned the room for the man in the bathrobe. There was no other way out of the room. He'd just vanished. Again. Or maybe he'd never really been there.

Like the ghostly key.

I ran my hand through my thick brown hair and wiped sweat from my forehead.

"Are you *trying* to get more detention time?" Holden asked.

"I . . . no. I thought I saw . . . didn't you see it?"

"See what?" Holden asked with growing impatience.

I didn't answer. I knew how crazy it would sound, because I was feeling pretty crazy.

She had no idea what I was talking about.

"Nothing," I said. "I thought I . . . never mind." I hurried to the upended desk and lifted it back into position. "Sorry."

I felt Holden staring at me. She must have been as confused as I was, though I wasn't sure if that was possible.

"Are you feeling all right, Mr. O'Mara?"

I wasn't even close to feeling all right.

"I'm fine," I said, and sat at my desk. "Sorry for that. I'll get back to homework."

Holden watched me for a second, then turned and went for the door. Halfway there she stopped, looked at me, then turned around and sat down at the teacher's desk. I think she wanted to keep an eye on me.

No problem. I didn't want to be alone anymore.

I opened my earth science book and took out a blank piece of paper. Holden must have thought I was going to take notes on magma. I wasn't. I wanted to draw something. A key. I wanted to re-create the image before I forgot the details. I quickly sketched the four-inch-long key that I had seen for only a moment before my hand passed through it. Below the drawing I wrote the phrase that made about as much sense as any of the impossible things I had just seen.

Or thought I had seen.

Surrender the key.

CHAPTER
2

"Detention?" my mother yelled in disbelief. "Again?"

She stood at the kitchen counter, holding a wooden pasta fork-spoon thing like a weapon. I thought she was going to wing it at me.

"The guy deserved it," I countered. "He was being a bully and—"

"I don't care if he stole your lunch money and made you stand on your head. You do not question the authority of your teachers."

"But he was embarrassing this girl."

Mom slammed the wooden fork down onto the counter so hard, I thought she'd break it. Or the counter.

"You realize these multiple detentions go on your permanent record."

"I'm in seventh grade. There is no permanent record."

"People remember. This kind of behavior is going to haunt you."

"Who's being haunted?" Dad asked brightly as he strolled into the kitchen.

I was, and it had nothing to do with Mr. Winser. But it wasn't a good time to mention a phantom bull or a spooky guy in a bathrobe. Adding insanity to their list of my flaws would make a bad night even worse.

"Your son was given a week of detention for talking back to a teacher," Mom said through pinched lips.

"Technically, I didn't say a word," I corrected.

"And now you're being flip with *us*!" Mom exclaimed. "This kind of behavior might make you a hero to your friends, but it's not going to help get you into a decent college."

"What's this got to do with college?" I shouted back in frustration. "I don't even want to go to college!"

The two went rigid and stared at me with stunned expressions, as if I had just told them I was getting a Batman logo tattooed across my forehead.

"I can't talk to you anymore," Mom said, and stormed away. She then stopped and spun back, stabbed a finger my way, and said, "You're grounded. Two weeks."

"I thought you couldn't talk to me anymore?" I said.

Thinking back, that probably wasn't the smartest thing to say.

Mom gasped in disbelief.

I did too. I'd crossed a line.

She glared at my dad as if it was all his fault, then turned and stomped out of the kitchen, leaving Dad and me alone for a long, awkward silence.

"Seriously?" he finally said, exasperated.

"I'm sorry. That was a dumb thing to say, but she never listens to my side."

"That crack about not going to college was uncalled for," he said.

"I know, I get it, but why does everything have to be about how it affects my future? Why can't I just live today?"

Dad sighed and went to the fridge to grab a can of soda.

"We're just looking out for you, Marcus. You're thirteen. Before you know it you'll be in high school, and after that, well, you really have to go to college."

"Jeez, Dad, I know. You've been drumming that into my head forever. But I'm not you. Or Mom. Maybe I want to do things differently."

Dad stared at his soda can for a good long time. I

think he was trying to come up with the right words. Or maybe he was just wishing he had cracked open a Sprite instead of a Pepsi.

"You know how much we love you, right?" he asked.

That was uncomfortable. Dad never said anything that sappy to me.

"Yeah," I said. Though I wasn't exactly sure how to measure love.

"Then let's all try to get along, okay?"

"Sure. Can you start by ungrounding me?"

"Sorry. Your mother and I always stand united."

"I know. I just wish you'd stand on my side for once."

I headed upstairs to my bedroom. There wouldn't be any dinner tonight. Mom had only gotten as far as taking out the pasta fork that she nearly clubbed me with. I was going to have to sneak down later for a little PB&J.

My parents cared about me. I knew that. Heck, if they hadn't wanted to have me, they wouldn't have, considering I was adopted. But sometimes I wondered what they expected. Did they want another human being in their lives? Or a robot they could dress up and mold into a clone of themselves?

I often thought about what my biological parents were like and if I was anything like them. There were times when I couldn't imagine having different parents. Other times I imagined (okay, hoped) I had parents who wouldn't be so obsessed with my permanent record and who might actually be proud of me for standing up to a bully, even if it was a teacher.

My mother was angry. Nothing new there; I was used to it. What I wasn't used to was hallucinating. That was a whole new territory.

What the heck happened at school?

I wished I could have talked to my parents about it. Most kids would have, I guess. But I didn't want them to think any less of me than they already did. Finding out I was a step away from an asylum would have made their brains melt.

I went to my bedroom and sat at my desk. Being grounded meant no TV and no computer. I knew the drill. I actually wished I hadn't done my homework during detention. It would have given me something to do other than stare at the walls, wondering if I was losing my mind. I grabbed my earth science book and slipped out the piece of paper with my sketch of the ghostly key.

" 'Surrender the key,' " I said out loud, reading the words that had been spelled out in bits of crushed glass. Or I *thought* had been spelled out in broken glass.

My sketch of the key was pretty accurate. I drew it to size, about four inches long. The handle had four ornate circles, like a four-leaf clover, with detailed carvings on each one. This sketch was the only physical record of the strange things I had seen that afternoon. Of course, I could just as easily have drawn a picture of Sasquatch, but that wouldn't prove Sasquatch was real.

I tacked the sketch to the corkboard above my desk, next to the various ticket stubs, video-game promos, and pictures I had on display. I was already resigning myself to the fact that I'd never find an explanation for what I'd seen. It was a fluke. A brain fart. An unexplainable incident that would soon become a distant memory.

And then I looked out my window.

Standing in our yard, staring up at me, was the man in the bathrobe. He slowly lifted his hand and gestured for me to come outside.

I pulled away from the window, practically flew across my room, and ran into the hallway. My pounding footsteps must have shaken the whole house, because my mother poked her head out of her bedroom door as I ran by.

"What are you doing?" she yelled, annoyed.

There was no time to stop and answer. I didn't want that guy to get away again. I thundered down the stairs and nearly knocked my dad over on my way to the door.

"Hey!" he shouted.

No time to stop. I threw open the door and shot outside.

"What do you want?" I yelled . . . to nobody.

The yard was empty.

I ran to the spot where he had been standing and spun around, but the guy was gone.

Mom and Dad were right on my heels.

"What in God's name?" Mom shouted as she ran up to me.

"What's going on, Marcus?" Dad asked.

I took one last, desperate look around.

"I—I . . . saw . . . ," I stammered. "There was a guy out here. He was looking up at me in the window."

"A guy?" Dad asked, glancing around.

"What do you mean, a guy?" Mom asked.

"A guy!" I shouted. "In pajamas."

Mom gave Dad a suspicious look. I knew what they were thinking, because I was thinking the same thing: there wasn't anybody there, and nobody could get away that fast.

"What are you doing, Marcus?" Mom asked in an exasperated tone that made my blood boil.

"*Doing?*" I shot back. "You think I'm making this up? Why would I do that?"

"I don't know," she said with frustration. "But there's nobody here."

I had seen him. He was real. But there was no use

trying to convince my parents of that, because the only thing it would prove was that I was crazy. I pushed past them and headed back to the house.

"And no TV!" Mom called after me.

She didn't have to say that. I think she liked pouring salt in my wounds.

All I wanted to do was sleep. I put on sweats and fell into bed but couldn't stop thinking about the guy, and the bull, and the fact that I was going out of my mind.

"'Surrender the key,'" I said aloud.

I wanted to surrender more than a phantom key. I wanted to surrender my memory of that entire day. I closed my eyes and rolled over to try and turn my brain off. It didn't take long before I had calmed down and my body relaxed. Sleep wasn't far off. There was nothing to prevent me from slipping into a state of unconsciousness . . .

. . . except for the strange scratching sound that came from under my bed.

CHAPTER
3

"That sounds kind of, like, I don't know, crazy," Lu said between bites of her tuna sandwich. "Cool but crazy."

Theo, Lu, and I had our own spot in the corner of the busy cafeteria, away from the lunchtime chaos.

"You say that like I don't already know," I said.

"All righty," Theo said. "We need to examine the facts."

Theo McLean, fact examiner. If I were harsh, I'd say he was a nerd, but it's not cool to put somebody down with labels. But man, he was a nerd. He was smart too. Straight-A smart. Except for gym.

We were like three different pieces of a very odd puzzle. Between Theo, a black guy who looked as though he should be rubbing elbows at a yacht club; Lu, with her Asian roller-derby-girl look, black tights, plaid shirts, and bold makeup; and me, a white guy who wore the same jeans and T-shirts every day until they were so stiff, they could stand up in the corner, we looked like the cast of some kids' show trying to cover all its ethnic bases. It would be a grand slam if we had a Hispanic friend. Or maybe a Tongan.

"What's to examine?" I said. "I saw things that weren't there."

"But what caused it?" Theo said thoughtfully while squeezing his earlobe the way he always did when he was thinking hard. "You were stressed because of the whole Winser thing."

"I wasn't stressed. I was triumphant."

"Yeah!" Lu exclaimed, and gave me a high five. "That was, like, awesome."

"Why was it *like* awesome?" Theo asked, irritated. "If it was *like* awesome, then it wasn't awesome. It was something else."

"So you're not, *like,* annoying?" Lu asked him. "You're just annoying?"

"Exactly!" Theo declared. "Wait, what?"

"Nerd."

"Can we get back to *my* problem?" I asked.

Theo continued in his best "I'm giving a lecture to those less gifted than me, so I must speak slowly and clearly" voice. "It's not just about Winser. You've been having issues with your parents."

"Issues? Is that what you call it? We're at each other's throats twenty-four seven."

"I'd call that an issue," Lu said with a wink.

"The mind is an amazing thing," Theo explained. "Maybe you're seeking shelter in some kind of fantasy that you know isn't real but offers a form of relief."

"How is being chased by a raging bull supposed to give me relief?"

"The bull could represent your mother," Theo explained, in full professor mode. "She's charging at you all the time. And the guy in the bathrobe could be your father. He's quiet most of the time, but it sounds like he's trying to communicate with you. Maybe give you a message."

Lu and I sat staring at Theo for a solid ten seconds.

"That's deep," Lu finally said. "Totally stupid, but deep."

"It's not stupid," Theo snapped. "You two are suggesting that something supernatural is going on here, but this isn't a horror movie. In real life there are always logical explanations."

"Maybe the logical explanation is that something supernatural is going on," Lu said, suddenly sounding very serious.

"I do not accept that!" Theo shot back angrily.

"Jeez, take it easy, professor," Lu said. "We're just trying to figure this out."

Theo had suddenly gotten really upset. I didn't know why. It wasn't like he was the one going through the weirdness. I stood up to put an end to the debate.

"Stop! You guys are no help," I said, and tossed my brown lunch bag into a distant trash bin. Three points.

"What are you going to do?" Lu asked me.

"Pretend like it didn't happen."

"What if you see something else weird?" Theo asked.

I shrugged. "I don't know. I guess it'll mean I'm, like . . . crazy. Or just plain crazy. Later."

I lied. I couldn't pretend as though it hadn't happened. For the rest of the day, my eyes kept wandering to classroom doors and windows. I was afraid that I might see the guy in the bathrobe. It was a good thing none of the teachers called on me, because I wasn't listening to anything they were saying.

When school ended, I showed up for my second day of detention. I was told to go to the computer lab, and when I got there, who did I see was my detention monitor?

Winser.

Great. Just what I needed.

"Four more days, Mr. O'Mara," he said without

making eye contact. "It'll give you time to think about how to change your belligerent attitude."

I didn't say a word. I had more things to worry about than sparring with an old bully with ugly neckties.

The computer lab was empty. Once again I was the only one in detention. What was up with that? Didn't anybody else in this school get in trouble?

"Use your time wisely," Winser said. "Go online and do homework. I have better things to do than babysit you."

With that, he left the room, and I was alone.

Yes! An hour of uninterrupted online time. There were two long rows of desks, with a laptop on each. I sat at one in the dead center, cracked my knuckles, and went to work. I started by going to some sports sites. From there I went to YouTube, but it was blocked. So were gaming sites. And Instagram. Block. Block. Block. The school made sure that any site worth going to was off-limits. Then I got an idea. Maybe it was desperate, but it was worth a shot. I went to Google, and in the search box I typed the words *Surrender the key.*

I hit Enter . . . and the computer screen instantly went blank.

Odd. I hit a few more keys, but nothing worked. I was about to flick the power switch to do a restart when the screen flashed back to life, along with all the others.

Each and every monitor flashed multiple images, as if a high-speed search engine had kicked in. I got fleeting glimpses of pictures, Web pages, and text that blew by in a blur. Then, one by one, the computers settled on a page. The same page. It started with the computers farthest away from me, followed by the others. Every computer stopped on the same Google search page.

The top result read: WEST SIDE MAN PLUNGES TO HIS DEATH FROM ROOF OF APARTMENT BUILDING.

It seemed as though some poor guy was killed when he jumped off a building in New York City. I clicked on the top search result. It was as if all the computers were synced up, because as soon as I hit the link, they all simultaneously changed to the same Web page.

It was a newspaper website. In bold letters the top headline read: FATAL PLUNGE! It was dated a few days ago. I scrolled down to read the following story:

> At approximately midnight on Friday, Michael Swenor, 33, a New York City firefighter, fell from the roof of the apartment building where he lived with his wife and young son. He was pronounced dead at the scene by paramedics, who were alerted by a 911 call. The incident is being investigated, though foul play is not suspected. Authorities are not ruling out suicide.

What a horrible thing. The guy died a nasty death, and nobody knew why.

I scrolled down to see a picture of the guy, and my heart stopped. At least, that was what it felt like. I threw myself back into the chair as if the picture were radioactive.

It was the guy in the bathrobe.

No mistake. It was a black-and-white shot of a guy in a firefighter's uniform, looking straight at me, just as he had in the classroom. And in my yard.

"O'Mara!" Winser shouted as he entered the room.

My computer screen instantly flipped and turned to fuzz. The other computers did too. *Pop! Pop! Pop!* I hadn't touched a thing, but they all started going snaky. One by one they winked off and went dark.

"Why are you messing with all the computers?" Winser asked gruffly as he hurried into the room.

"I . . . I'm not," I said, trying to keep my brain from going as wonky as the computers. "I was only working on this one."

Winser went to one of the computers and tried to power it up. It wouldn't start. He tried another. And another. Nothing.

"They're all fried," Winser said, his anger rising. "What did you do?"

"I didn't do anything!" I shouted. "Honest! They all just turned on by themselves!"

"Unacceptable!" Winser declared.

I was in deep trouble. I was going to have to face his wrath, and the wrath of the principal. A huge storm was about to hit that was sure to follow me home. But none of that mattered. All I could think about was the face of the guy in the newspaper. The guy in the bathrobe.

He was real.

He had a name.

Michael Swenor.

And he was dead.

CHAPTER
4

The fury of Winser was unleashed.

On me.

I doubted if he even cared about the computers. It was all about payback because I made him look bad in front of the class. He reported the computer crash to the principal. The principal reported it to my parents, and suddenly I was suspended from school for a day. I can't say they didn't listen to my side of the story. They did. They just didn't believe it.

I wouldn't have believed it either if I hadn't seen it for myself.

"What do you have to say for yourself?" Mom asked.

My parents sat next to each other on the couch across from me in our living room. Mom didn't seem angry.

That was bad. It meant she was beyond angry. Dad kept rubbing the back of his head as if massaging his brain would somehow help him solve the problem of what to do with his delinquent son.

"I'm telling the truth," I said with no emotion. "I was only using one of the computers when they all went bat-snack crazy."

"By magic," my mother said with total skepticism.

"Maybe" was my reply. "I don't know what else to say."

I decided not to tell them the whole truth. If they didn't believe computers could turn themselves on, they sure as heck wouldn't believe I was getting a message from the great beyond about the ghost of a dead fire-fighter who was haunting me.

But I had a plan to try to figure out what really happened. To pull it off, I was going to have to take my punishment without complaining.

"What are we going to do with you, Marcus?" my mother asked, exasperated.

My first instinct was to shout out, *Do? You don't have to do anything!* But I bit my tongue.

"I'm sorry you don't believe me, Mom," I said, trying to sound all calm and rational. "I get that it doesn't make sense. It doesn't make sense to me either, but it's the truth. I guess there's nothing I can say to explain what happened, so I'll just have to take my punishment tomorrow and try to make things better with Winser. I mean, Mr. Winser."

The two stared at me, looking as befuddled about my not fighting back as they were about the computer snafu.

"Well, that's good to hear, Marcus," Dad said with a little uncertainty. "Very mature of you."

"I'm trying," I said with as much sincerity as I could fake.

Mom looked back and forth between the two of us with confusion. She wasn't sure if she should buy my sudden retreat, but I was saying the exact right things, so it wasn't as though she could argue.

"That's all we're asking for," Dad said.

"You know what? Having a day alone to think about what happened might be exactly the kind of therapy I need," I said.

"Oh please," Mom said sarcastically.

Even Dad wasn't buying that one.

"Don't go laying it on too thick," he said. "Let's just agree to move past this and have a fresh start when you go back to school."

"Got it," I said. "Done."

Mom wanted to say more. She was all set to lay into me again about what a disappointment I'd turned out to be. But since I had basically rolled over and agreed to be a good boy, I'd taken the wind out of her anger sails.

"And absolutely no TV tomorrow," she commanded, just to prove she was still calling the shots. "This isn't a vacation day."

"I promise I will not turn the TV on," I said. I meant it too. "I won't even go online unless it's for schoolwork."

Mom was ready to argue, because that was how all our conversations went. She opened her mouth, ready to fight, but it must have suddenly hit her that I had totally agreed to her demands without question, so she backed off.

"Oh" was all she managed to say. "Good."

"Great! Good talk," Dad declared, and stood up. "What's for dinner?"

He headed for the kitchen, leaving Mom and me alone.

She stared at me in silence. I wished I could have told her the truth. I wished I could have said that impossible things were happening and I was scared. I wanted her to be able to make it all better. But neither of us was in the business of making things better for each other lately.

"I really will try, Mom" was all I said.

"I guess we'll have to see," she said dismissively, and got up to follow Dad.

If only she knew what I was really planning to do

the next day, the roof would have blown off the house. Both my parents would be leaving for work early in the morning. Mom worked at Stony Brook Hospital, and Dad took the train into New York City. I had made that trip on the commuter train many times, when Dad took me to work or we went into the city as a family. I knew the drill. But I had never made the trip on my own.

That was about to change. I was going to go into New York City alone, to track down a ghost.

I had trouble sleeping that night as my mind wrestled with a slew of impossible questions. Were ghosts real? Was I being haunted? Why? Who was this Michael Swenor dude? And if he was a ghost, why was he bothering me? It was actually a relief to know I wasn't going totally off my nut. Michael Swenor was a real person. Dead, but real.

I had to find out why he was haunting me.

The next morning I waited until my parents left for work before jumping on my bike and riding to the Stony Brook station with a pocketful of lawn-mowing money to catch a train from Stony Brook, Connecticut, to New York City . . . where Michael Swenor had lived and died.

Dad caught the 7:02 express every morning. I couldn't risk taking the same train, so I bought my round-trip ticket at the window and waited for the 7:19. It was a chilly October morning, and all I had on to keep me warm was a hoodie. I had to pace on the train platform to keep the blood circulating, which probably annoyed the heck out of all the half-asleep commuters. Too bad. I was cold, and too nervous to stand still, anyway. I had never done anything like this before, and, to be honest, I was a little nervous. Okay, a lot nervous. It's easy making a trip like this when your parents handle all the decisions and all you have to do is keep up with them. Now I was on my own.

The train trip was like riding in a library. Everybody sat quietly, in their own little world. Most everyone read the *New York Times* or focused on their cell phones and tablets. The rest slept. I plugged in my earbuds and settled in to listen to music to keep calm.

As the train rolled closer to the city, I noticed one person who stood out from the rest of the business-suit-wearing, newspaper-reading, half-asleep passengers. It was an old lady. She sat several rows in front of me in a seat facing backward, so I was able to get a good look at her. She seemed ancient but not frail. She wore a black shawl over a dark-green dress that went down to her ankles. Her gray hair was done up in some old-fashioned 'do that was piled on top of her head like a hornet's nest. On her lap was an old leather book that could have been from the 1800s. Come to think of it, she looked like she could have been from the 1800s too. She read her book with a pinched expression. The word *sour* came to mind. I imagined that was what my mother would look like in fifty years.

I couldn't take my eyes off her, mostly because she was so out of place. I wondered what she was doing there. Maybe she was going to a museum. Or maybe she worked at a museum, probably as one of the exhibits. I kept staring at her until she suddenly raised her eyes and stared right back at me.

Whoa! It was as if she knew I was watching. I didn't look away at first. I couldn't. Her gaze had me transfixed. She stared right into my eyes and smiled. It wasn't a warm, grandmotherly expression either. She had a twisted grimace that said *I know you've been looking at me, sonny boy.*

I quickly looked out the window and didn't dare glance back at her for the rest of the trip, for fear that she was still staring at me. When the train arrived and everyone got up, I finally stole a look her way. Thankfully, she was gone, but the experience left me strangely creeped out.

Once off the train I found myself in a sea of people flooding into Grand Central Terminal. Everybody but me seemed to know exactly where they were going. It was like getting caught in the white water of a fast-moving river. Whenever I stopped to get my bearings, people had to skirt around me, usually with a huff because I had dared to throw off their rhythm. Too bad. I was on a mission. I had Googled Michael Swenor's address the night before and found out that he had lived in Greenwich Village. It was too far to walk, and I didn't know how to hail a cab, so I plotted out a route using the subway. From there it would be a short walk to the scene of the crime. Or the accident. Or the suicide. Or whatever it was. My hope was that somebody might be home who could tell me something about Michael Swenor and why he might be haunting me.

It all looked so easy on the map I'd printed out. Trying to do it while being bumped around by a thousand people rushing in every direction was a different deal. But I couldn't let that freak me out. This was my chance. Maybe my only chance.

I found the stairs that led to the underground station and hurried down, searching for a ticket booth. It was total chaos. I bumped into a few dozen people and got more than one dirty look. Finally, I spotted a long row of machines where people were buying tickets. I walked up to one and stared at the wall of buttons, trying to decipher the code, when I sensed somebody walk up behind me.

"Need some help?" came a friendly voice.

I turned around to see who had come to my rescue, and caught my breath.

It was the old lady from the train.

I stood with my mouth open in disbelief. She seemed much less stern than before. I wouldn't say she was a kindly old lady, but at least she didn't freeze me with a look that made me want to cry.

"These silly machines aren't as complicated as they look," she said. "Where is it you're going?"

"Uh . . . Fourteenth Street," I said numbly.

"Of course you are," she said with a knowing smile, as if she had expected me to say that.

Odd.

"Choose a single-ride ticket and put your money in. Easy as pie."

I nodded dumbly, turned to the machine, and did just that. A paper card dropped into the trough below, along with a bunch of dollar coins in change. I gathered it all up, then turned back to the woman.

"Thanks," I said. "I wasn't sure how to—"

She was gone. I looked around for her, but she had already melted into the crowd.

"You done?" a guy behind me asked impatiently.

"Uh, yeah, sure. Sorry, chief," I said.

I left the machine, used the card to get through

the turnstile, and found the stairs that led down to the trains. When I hit the platform, I quickly walked to the far end, where there weren't any people. I never liked being in a crowd when a train came in. I always felt as though I might get jostled and pushed onto the track. I know, paranoid, but what can you do? I stood inside the yellow safety strip on the floor that cautioned people from getting too close to the edge and gazed into the dark tunnel, hoping the train would come soon. I wanted to get there, learn what I could, and then beat it back home before Mom and Dad realized I wasn't in my room doing prison time.

Part of me feared that this adventure would be a risky waste of time. I was looking for answers but didn't know what questions to ask. What if I met Michael Swenor's wife? What would I say? "Funny thing, Mrs. Swenor, your husband's ghost is haunting me. How's your day going otherwise?"

This was beginning to feel like a really bad idea.

The headlight of an oncoming train appeared deep within the tunnel. This was it. The last leg of my trip. I was at the very end of the platform, so when the train arrived it was still moving fast. I took a nervous step back to be sure I was completely clear of the oncoming vehicle. Looking directly ahead, I saw my own reflection in its moving windows as the first car flew by. There was a short break as the tail sped past, followed by the next car. When the next window moved past, I saw my reflection again.

Except now somebody was standing directly behind me.

It was the old woman.

I tensed up. Where had she come from?

"Surrender the key," she whispered into my ear.

"Wha—?"

I felt a shove from behind. Or maybe it was my natural reaction to get away. Whatever it was, I stumbled forward, directly toward the moving train. I quickly realized what was happening and threw my leg out to stop myself. My foot landed way beyond the safety strip, but I was able to stop my momentum, with my head only a few inches from the hurtling train.

I pushed myself back and away from danger while spinning to face the old woman.

"Why did you do that?" I screamed.

She wasn't there.

There was nowhere for her to have gone, yet the platform was empty.

People looked at me as if I were one of those nutjobs who walk around yelling at nobody, because that was exactly what I was doing.

My heart was racing. What had happened? Was she

another hallucination? Hallucinations can't shove people. But did she really push me? Or had I leapt forward out of surprise?

The train finally rolled to a stop, and the doors slid open. I jumped inside and plunked myself down in the seat opposite the door, praying she wouldn't get on. A few seconds later the bell rang, the door slid closed, and we began to roll.

I took a deep breath to try to calm down.

Surrender the key.

That was exactly what she said. The same words that were spelled out in glass at school. I couldn't help but think it might not have been a coincidence that she was on the commuter train this morning, and in the subway. And on the platform.

She was following me.

The train picked up speed. As my car rolled past the platform, I saw that one person was still standing there.

The old woman stood by herself, clutching her black shawl, staring me square in the eye.

CHAPTER
5

My GPS got me right to the brownstone apartment building where Michael Swenor lived. Or used to live. I was lucky to find it without getting lost, because the whole way all I could think about was that pinched old lady who tried to push me into the speeding train.

Surrender the key.

Was she a ghost too? She sure popped in and out quickly enough. That's not exactly normal. Or human.

I looked down at the sidewalk. Was I standing on the very spot where Michael Swenor had hit the ground? The thought gave me the creeps, so I jumped away and ran up the cement steps to the front door. Inside was an entryway with another door, which led to the lobby. That second door was locked. I scanned the row of buttons on the wall. Each had a name and an apartment number next to it. There was only one that mattered.

Swenor. Apartment 4B. Top floor.

I hesitated. What if Mrs. Swenor was there? What would I say to her? She wasn't going to feel like talking to a crazy kid about her husband's ghost. I actually took a step back, ready to run the heck out of there, but forced myself to stop. The fear of not knowing why I was being haunted was even scarier than facing a sad lady.

I pressed the button next to her name.

Five seconds passed. Maybe nobody was home. Or maybe she was in the shower. I didn't want to buzz again, because that would be rude. I waited a few more seconds, wondering if I should take off, when the speaker came to life.

"Yes?" came a woman's small, frail voice. It sounded as though she had just woken up.

My throat closed. Just as well. I hadn't thought of what I was going to say, anyway.

"Is someone there?" she asked.

"M-Mrs. Swenor?" I said meekly.

"Can I help you?" she asked, now sounding more awake and a little irritated.

"I hope so," I said tentatively. "You don't know me, but—"

"I'm not talking to any more reporters," she said curtly. "Go away."

"I'm not a reporter," I said quickly, as if grasping for a lifeline that was being pulled out of reach. "My name's Marcus O'Mara. I live in—"

A harsh buzzer sound made me jump. It came from the inside door. It took a second for me to realize she was letting me in. I leapt for the door, grabbed the knob, and pulled it open. There was no turning back now. I walked quickly to the elevator and rode the creaky old box up to the fourth floor. Apartment 4B was at the end of a long, dark hallway. I stepped up to the door and was about to knock when it opened slowly.

My knees went rubbery. I hadn't really thought I would get as far as this, and I went into total brain lock.

Mrs. Swenor peeked around the door. She was probably younger than my mother but looked a lot older. Her eyes were—I don't know, hollow. I guess grief over losing your husband will do that. She wore gray NYU sweats and had her hair pulled back into a ponytail.

"Mrs. Swenor?" I asked tentatively.

When she focused on me, her face lit up. She actually broke out in a smile.

"Oh, Liam," she said as she pulled the door open. She stepped forward quickly and wrapped her arms around me to give me a hug.

I don't know what I was expecting from her, but it sure wasn't that. I didn't hug back. I didn't know the lady, and I sure as heck wasn't Liam.

Awkward.

She pulled back and held me at arm's length. She was crying, but her tears seemed more like tears of joy than of sorrow because she kept smiling.

"Come in," she said, and pulled me inside.

This felt totally wrong, but I was too stunned to do anything but go along. She led me down a short hallway and into the living room of the warm and homey apartment.

"Sit," she said as she brought me to a big old couch. "I want to take a good look at you."

She didn't let go of my hands as we both sat. The whole time, she kept looking me straight in the eye.

"I think you made a mistake," I said. "My name isn't Liam."

She smiled warmly. "I know. It's Marcus, right?"

"Yeah, and we've never met before. I'm here because . . ."

I stopped myself. I couldn't bring myself to say the crazy words.

"It's okay," she said kindly. "Tell me."

"It's not going to make sense."

Mrs. Swenor turned serious. "Marcus, I promise, there's nothing you could say that would surprise me."

She wiped her eyes and gave me a pleasant smile.

"I . . . I'm sorry about your husband," I said, figuring that was the best way to start.

"Thank you. Do you know anything about him?"

What I wanted to say was *Absolutely. His ghost has been haunting me! Does that count?* But that wouldn't have been cool.

"Not really" was my answer.

"Would you like to?"

"Uh, yeah," I said with relief.

"Michael was a great person. A firefighter. The kind of guy who was always the first to run into a burning building." She took a deep, sad breath. "I worried that something terrible would happen to him at work. I never imagined that the terrible thing could happen right here at home."

"I'm sorry" was all I could think of saying.

She got herself back together and continued. "Michael also had a hobby. I guess that's what you'd call it. He investigated paranormal events."

I sat bolt upright.

"Really?"

"It was mostly online research. It wasn't like he was traveling around to haunted houses or anything. It was all done right here. So many times he'd come bursting out of his office, all excited because he'd solved a mystery about how someone died or why a house was haunted."

Her voice trailed off as if the memories she was digging up were painful. "That was a long time ago," she finally said. "Twelve years. He suddenly stopped and never mentioned another word about anything to do with the paranormal."

"Why did he stop?" I asked.

Her pained expression made me feel as though she had something to say that wouldn't be easy.

"Michael had a partner. His best friend. They did the investigations together. I liked him. His wife too. We were all good friends."

Her voice caught as if she was fighting back a wave of sad memories.

"Why did you call me Liam?" I asked, trying to get her mind onto something else.

She smiled as if remembering better times. "Because that's who you are."

"No, I'm not."

"But you are. I've known you since you were a baby."

My head started to spin. Was this lady off her nut?

She added, "Besides, you look just like your father."

"Wha—? You know my father?" I exclaimed, my heart racing.

"I do. He was the friend of my husband's I told you about."

I jumped to my feet.

"No way!" I shouted. "My father's not a . . . a . . . ghostbuster. If you really knew him, you'd know how impossible that is."

"I'm not talking about Ed O'Mara," she said.

"But that's my father," I shot back.

"I know. Your adoptive father. I'm talking about your biological father."

The rush of adrenaline nearly knocked me over.

"You knew my real father?" I exclaimed.

"Your mother too. They were our best friends. Michael was so upset when they died that he completely stopped his investigations. He was done with it all . . . until last week. Something happened that scared him, Marcus. He kept saying that it was back and it was real."

"What was back?" I asked.

"He wouldn't tell me."

I was getting dizzy and had to sit back down.

"There's more," Mrs. Swenor said. "Michael kept saying he had to tell someone about what had happened. Someone special. But he never got the chance."

"Who was it?" I asked.

"He said he had to tell you, Marcus."

"Jim and Joan Roxbury," Mrs. Swenor said as she handed me a picture. "Your parents."

It was a photo of two smiling people, a man and a woman, with their arms around one another. The man was holding up bunny-ear fingers behind the woman's head. What was so incredible about the picture— besides *everything*—was that the guy looked exactly like an older version of me. He had my same dark hair and eyes. The woman was tall, with blond hair that fell to her shoulders. Both looked tan and happy.

They were my parents. My *real* parents.

I was relieved, excited, curious, and more than a little bit sad.

"So my real name is Liam Roxbury?"

"No, your real name is Marcus O'Mara. Liam was the name your birth parents gave you."

"I knew that they died, but nobody told me how," I said. "Do you know?"

She nodded and took a deep breath. I felt bad for her because I was asking her to relive more painful memories. But heck, I had to know!

"They were on their sailboat in the Atlantic. They loved sailing. A storm came up quickly. The boat capsized. They were both presumed to have drowned."

"Presumed?" I asked.

"Their bodies were never recovered."

Wow. Grim.

"You were a year old. We thought of adopting you, but Michael and I were just too young. And Michael was torn up over Jim's death. It wasn't a good time to bring a baby into our lives."

"Weren't there any relatives to take me?"

"None. You were put up for adoption, and that's when the O'Maras came into the picture. But I didn't lose track of you. I wanted to make sure you had gone to a good family, and you did."

I kept staring at the picture. My worries about being haunted didn't matter much anymore. I was looking at my parents. My real parents.

"So I do know you, at least a little," Mrs. Swenor said. "Now it's your turn. Why are you here?"

All my worries came flooding back. I put the picture down and took a deep breath to buy time and try to kick my brain into gear.

She must have sensed that I was having trouble, because she said again, "There's nothing you could say that would surprise me."

"Don't bet on that."

She stared at me, waiting for me to say something.

"I've been," I said, stumbling over my own thoughts and words, "I've been seeing things. Strange things."

Her gaze didn't waver, so I let it all out in a rush of verbal diarrhea.

"There was a bull, and an old lady, and things were smashed one second but not the next. I'm not sure what was real and what wasn't, because I'm the only one who's been seeing it."

I stole a look at her, expecting her to roll her eyes or reach for the phone to call an ambulance to cart the loony kid away.

She didn't.

"This is the tough part," I said. "I saw your husband. At least, I think it was him. Or his ghost. That's why I'm here."

Mrs. Swenor didn't show any emotion. I think she was trying to absorb the crazy information.

"Did he say anything?" she asked with a shaky voice.

It was the only hint that I was getting through to her . . . and that she didn't think I was nuts.

"No. He just held out this old-fashioned key and—"

Mrs. Swenor gasped and sat back so suddenly, it was as if somebody had shoved her.

"You sure it was a key?" she asked, her voice trembling.

"Well, yeah. I tried to grab it, but my hand went through it like it was, well, a ghost. And there were messages too. They said—"

"Surrender the key," she said softly.

It was my turn to sit back.

"How did you know?"

Mrs. Swenor's hands trembled. She ran them through her hair nervously, as if that would somehow stop the shaking.

"When Michael started acting strangely, I tried to get him to open up about it, but the most I got from him was that he had to do something else but was afraid it might be another mistake."

"Another mistake? Did he make more than one?"

"I don't know. All he kept saying was that he had to protect me, and the less I knew, the better."

"Did he say what he had to do?"

"Yes. Apparently, twelve years ago, right before your parents went on that sailing trip, Jim gave my husband something for safekeeping. He asked Michael to take care of it until the time was right."

"Right for what?" I asked.

Mrs. Swenor looked straight at me and said, "To give it to you."

I gasped. At least I think I did. That's usually what happens when you hear something that is so stunning, you have trouble breathing.

"My father gave your husband something for me twelve years ago?"

Mrs. Swenor stood and grabbed her purse from the floor next to the couch. She reached inside and pulled out a ring of keys. She flipped through them until she came upon one that was small and golden.

"That's not it," I said, actually feeling relieved.

She went to a table next to the couch. The table had a drawer; the drawer had a lock. Mrs. Swenor inserted the key with shaking hands, twisted it, and pulled the drawer open.

My heart was beating so fast, I was sure she could hear it.

She reached inside and gently lifted out a thin leather cord. Dangling from it was a four-inch-long brass key.

The key.

"Your father asked Michael to give this to you, but only when the time was right. I think that time is now."

"Noooo!" came a scream from deeper in the apartment.

We both looked with surprise toward the hallway to see a little boy sprinting toward us. Before we could react, the kid ran into the room and snatched the key from her.

"You can't have it!" he yelled, and ran back the way he had come.

"Alec!" Mrs. Swenor yelled.

He ran into a room at the end of the hall and slammed the door shut.

"This has been so hard for him. He was on the roof with Michael when—"

"I get it," I said, and took off after the kid.

It was a totally brazen move. He wasn't my brother, and this wasn't my house. But if my real father wanted me to have that key, nobody was going to keep it from me.

CHAPTER
7

It was pretty bold of me to run down the hallway of a stranger's apartment, but I didn't think twice about it.

"Hey, Alec?" I called. "It's cool. Let's talk about it."

I pushed open his bedroom door and poked my head in, only to see that things were definitely *not* cool.

The window leading out to the fire escape was open. I caught a quick glimpse of Alec's sneakered feet as he climbed up the ladder outside.

Headed for the roof.

"Hey!" I shouted, and ran straight for the window.

It didn't seem safe for a little kid to be crawling around on a fire escape. It didn't seem all that safe for me either. But I crawled right out the window and looked up to see Alec stepping off the steel structure and onto the roof.

"Alec!" I called. I don't know why. It wasn't as though he was going to stop and come back just because I yelled his name.

I climbed up after him, and when I'd gotten halfway up, I heard the window slam shut below me. I looked down and saw Mrs. Swenor inside, pulling on it, trying to get it open. For some reason the window had slid shut and was now stuck.

I was on my own.

I quickly climbed up, trying not to think about how this was the very same roof that Michael Swenor had fallen from. When I got to the top, I saw Alec running to the far side.

"Alec, stop!" I yelled.

"You can't have it!" he shouted back.

I climbed onto the roof and walked after him. I didn't want to panic the kid. I was up there to make sure he didn't get hurt, not to run him off the roof.

Oh yeah, and to get the key.

As I strode across the tar-papered surface, the wind picked up. A dark line of storm clouds was creeping in from the west. No biggie. We wouldn't be up here long enough to get caught in the rain.

Alec reached the far side and turned to face me. Tears ran down his cheeks.

"It's okay," I said, trying to sound calm. "My name's Marcus. Your father knew my father and—"

"I know who you are," Alec said, sobbing. "You can't have the key."

He clutched the brass key and folded his arms together.

The wind grew stronger. The line of storm clouds drew closer. Fast. Really fast. Suddenly, the roof was cast into shadow. I looked over my shoulder and saw another line of dark clouds looming in from the exact opposite direction. Huh? There were two lines of ominous black clouds racing toward each other.

"I'm sorry about your dad, Alec," I said. "I hear he was a really good guy."

His tears came even harder.

"He followed me up here to save me," Alec cried.

"Tell me what happened."

"The dog. It was under my bed. It chased me here, to the edge. Right here. I saw a ladder, but when I climbed over, it wasn't there anymore. It was a . . . a . . ."

"An illusion," I said with a growing sense of dread. I didn't like where this was going for all sorts of reasons.

Alec nodded. He was spewing impossible facts . . . that I knew were totally possible.

"It was the lady," he said, sobbing. "She tried to make me fall."

I stopped breathing.

"Lady?" I asked, stunned. "What lady?"

"An old lady," he said. "With long gray hair."

It felt as though I'd been punched in the stomach.

"In a green dress?" I asked, incredulous.

Alec nodded. "Nobody believes me."

I didn't know whether to cry or scream or puke or all three. What happened to Michael Swenor wasn't an accident. Or a suicide.

It was her.

"I believe you," I said numbly.

"She is very bad."

"Yeah, I'm getting that."

"My daddy saved me," Alec said through hitching breaths. "But then the dog came back. It knocked him over the side."

The stiff wind picked up and began to howl. I had to plant my feet wider apart, or I might have been blown off the roof. Alec crouched down and pushed himself against the low safety wall for protection.

"That key belonged to my father," I said. "Your dad wanted me to have it."

"No!" Alec cried. "It was *my* father's!"

Lightning flashed through the clouds, followed by

a sharp clap of thunder. The two storm fronts had collided, blocking out every last bit of blue sky. The dense, dark canopy had turned day into night.

I knelt down a few feet from Alec.

"Let's go downstairs and talk about it," I said, trying to sound calm, but it wasn't easy while screaming to be heard over the howling wind.

"No!" he yelled. "I'm keeping it forever and—"

He spotted something over my shoulder, and his eyes went wide.

"No, not again," he said, so low I could barely hear it.

I spun around to see what he was looking at.

A woman stood on the far side of the roof.

Not Mrs. Swenor.

Her.

The old woman's long green dress and black shawl snapped in the wind. Her gray hair was no longer piled on top of her head. Long, loose tendrils flew around her head in a swirling maelstrom that looked like gray fire.

It made my blood run cold.

"Is that her?" I yelled to Alec.

Alec managed to nod.

I stood up to face the woman.

"Who are you?" I yelled. "What do you want?"

She didn't move. Good thing. If she'd taken a step closer, I think I would have passed out.

"She wants the key," Alec called to me. "I won't let her have it either."

"Did you hear that?" I called to her. "You aren't getting the key."

A brilliant bolt of lightning tore through the sky, followed by a huge rumble of thunder. It was as if my announcement had angered the gods.

We couldn't stay on this roof forever, but the only way down was to go past that old creep. It was a standoff. Both of us were waiting for the other to blink.

I saw movement along the edge of the safety wall behind the old lady. At first I thought it was a shadow, but there was no sunlight to make one. A dark mass rose up and crept over the edge of the roof.

"What is that?" Alec asked nervously.

It looked like thick, molten tar. It oozed up over the edge of the safety wall and slid down until it hit the surface of the roof. From there it kept moving and growing. It stretched out for several yards along the roof behind the old lady while flowing forward, spreading toward us. When it reached the woman, it split and skirted around her as if it could think and knew she was there. It then joined back together in front of her, leaving the old lady on a clean, dry island.

Either the nasty blob had a mind of its own, or she was controlling it.

Alec scrambled to my side and leaned into me for security.

I wished I had somebody to lean into.

"I'm scared," he said.

Join the club.

The dark pool now covered half the roof and continued to spread forward, moving ever closer to us.

I looked back over the edge of the roof behind us, desperate to find a way to escape.

This time I saw it.

There was a metal ladder attached to the side of the building.

"There's a ladder," I said to Alec. "I'll go down first. You follow right behind me."

"No!" he screamed. "It's not real."

In my growing panic I'd forgotten about the illusions.

The old lady smiled at me as if she knew how close I'd come to going over the edge. She lifted up her hand and opened her palm in a gesture that meant only one thing.

Surrender the key.

The wind howled as the black ooze grew closer. What was it? Would it burn us? Was it a black hole that would suck us into a bottomless pit? Or would it catch our feet in its stickiness and drag us over the edge?

"Maybe we should give it to her," Alec said with fear.

Thunder rumbled as lightning ripped through the clouds.

The woman stood with her hand outstretched, unwavering.

The ooze was only a few yards from us and flowing closer with each passing second. I looked back to the ladder.

It wasn't there anymore. It had never been there. It was an illusion.

Knowing that actually gave me an idea.

"I think we're okay!" I shouted to Alec. "None of this is real."

"Are you sure?" he asked tentatively.

No, I wasn't. But it wasn't as though I had another plan. I stood up straight and called out to the old lady, "You're not getting the key."

It was a huge risk. Giving her the key would probably save us. But did we really need to be saved?

"Here," Alec said.

He held the key out to me. It dangled from the leather cord the same way as when his father had held it out to me. His ghost father.

"Better you have it than her," he added.

A twisted bolt of lightning blasted through the sky, followed by a gut-rumbling clap of thunder.

I looked to the old woman and saw something new.

Her expression had changed.

She looked angry.

The black ooze was only a few feet from us. A putrid rotten-egg smell wafted from it and stuck in the back of my throat, making me gag. The wind blew even harder. If it got any stronger, we wouldn't have to worry about the black ick anymore. We'd be blown over the edge.

Alec clutched the leather cord in his small fist. The key on the other end was swept up by the wind, pulling the cord parallel to the roof.

I gave one last look at the old woman.

"No way," I said defiantly. "This belonged to my father."

I reached out and grabbed the key.

"Now it's mine."

It felt warm in my hand, as if being there was absolutely right.

The woman didn't agree. She threw her head back and let out an unearthly bellow that sounded like a mixture of pain and anger so powerful that it made the roof tremble.

"Look!" Alec exclaimed, pointing to the sky.

The clouds were breaking up, allowing sunshine to peek through.

The wind died quickly, its shrieking faded to silence.

The rooftop was slowly bathed in warm golden light from above.

More important, the black pool was gone.

So was the old lady.

"Alec!" called Mrs. Swenor as she climbed up onto the roof.

Alec ran to meet his mom. She dropped to her knees as he slammed into her, nearly knocking her over. The two hugged as if neither would ever let go.

"I couldn't open the window," she cried, the tears flowing. "What were you thinking? Why did you come up here?"

"I was thinking about Daddy," Alec said with confidence. "This was the last place I was with him. I thought maybe he'd tell me what to do."

"Never, ever come up here again, do you understand?" she scolded.

"I won't have to," Alec said. "I gave the key to Marcus. I think it's where it belongs now."

The two looked up at me.

I felt the weight of the large key in my hand.

"I don't know what that key is," Mrs. Swenor said, "or

why it's so important. But your father wanted Michael to give it to you, so now it's yours."

"Thank you" was all I could think to say.

"Promise me one thing?" she asked.

"What's that?"

"Be very, very careful."

CHAPTER
8

The whole way back home, I kept looking over my shoulder in case the old lady was creeping up on me. In the subway station I pressed my back to the wall for fear she'd leap out of nowhere and shove me onto the tracks. On the train to Connecticut, I stared at my feet, afraid I'd catch her reflection in one of the windows.

Who was she? *What* was she? A witch? Another ghost? Why did she want the key so bad? It was just a key. A tool. The real question was, what did the key unlock?

The only good thing that came out of the whole mess was that I discovered who my real parents were. Jim and Joan Roxbury. They died in a sailboat accident when I was a year old.

And, oh yeah, my real father's hobby was investigating the paranormal. Let's not forget that. As much as I wondered about my biological parents and hoped I might be a perfect replica of them, never in my wildest dreams did I imagine that my father would be a ghost hunter who would reach out to me from beyond the grave. Didn't see that one coming.

As I rode my bike home from the Stony Brook station, I made a decision. I was tired of dealing with this on my own. I had to tell my parents what was going on. Maybe they'd think I was crazy, but I was willing to take that chance, because I needed help from someone, and they were the most likely candidates.

I finally rolled up to our house at four o'clock, a solid hour before Mom got home from work . . .

. . . except for today. When I turned into the driveway, I saw her car parked in front of the garage.

Uh-oh.

She had just pulled up and was climbing out when she spotted me. Her face fell instantly. There was a short moment of suspended animation as the two of us stood there, staring at each other, waiting for somebody to make the first move.

"Seriously?" she said through clenched teeth.

I knew she was still angry about the suspension,

but now she'd found out that I had taken off instead of spending the day at home in leg irons. This was not going to go well. I had to be careful about what I said. How much did she really know? I didn't want to lie to her, but if I told her that I'd been to the city before she heard the whole story, she'd never trust me again.

I shrugged as if it was no big deal and said, "I didn't think the suspension was supposed to last all day."

"Why, Marcus?" she asked.

"Why what?"

"Why do you always do the exact opposite of what I ask?"

"I don't," I argued, not too strongly, and left it at that.

"But you do," she said with frustration. "What is your deal? Do you take some odd pleasure from disobeying us? Do you actually like fighting? Is there a switch in your head that flips every time we ask you to do something, that makes you do the exact opposite of what we ask? Do you like seeing me angry? Help me out here. I want to know."

"Really, Mom? Do you really think everything I do is about making you angry?"

"I have no idea why you do the things you do," she said, exasperated.

I should have let it go. Truth was, she had caught me

doing something wrong. But her anger wasn't just about today. It had been building up for a long time, and I felt as though I had to defend myself.

"Well, maybe I'm just not the kind of kid you wanted," I said.

I figured that would guilt her into backing off.

It didn't.

"Maybe you aren't," she said.

Her words hit me like a punch to the gut.

The shocked expression on her face made it seem as though she was just as surprised that those words had come out of her mouth as I was. But, shock or no, she had said them.

"That's what I figured," I said. I dropped my bike and pushed past her, headed for the door.

"Marcus, come back here," she called after me.

I kept going, stormed into the house and up the stairs. I wanted to slam the bedroom door shut behind me, but that would have only added fuel to the fire. Any thoughts I had about confiding in my parents about what I was going through were blown up in those few minutes. My biggest fear had proved to be true. She'd finally admitted it.

Whenever they looked at me, all they saw was one big disappointment.

I pulled out my cell phone, thinking I'd call Lu or

Theo to unload, but threw the phone onto my bed. That was a conversation that needed to be had in person. I sat down on the bed, not knowing what to do next, my leg pumping with angry energy.

It didn't take long to figure it out.

I reached into my hoodie pocket and grasped the key, waiting a few seconds before pulling it out. Examining this key was the next step on this adventure. It might possibly tell me more about my father and mother. My *real* father and mother.

I pulled the key out, opened my fingers, and stared at the piece of metal that lay across my palm. It was made of brass that was dark from tarnish. I guess the one word I could use to describe it was *fancy*. And *old-fashioned*. Okay, that's two words. The part that was inserted into the lock was complicated, with many intricate ridges and points. This key fit into only one lock, but which one? It was definitely something from a long time ago, like the big old door of a castle or a giant pirate's chest. It didn't look as though it would fit anything that was made in this century. Or the last.

This key was as much a trophy as it was a tool. The shaft was engraved with an ocean-wave pattern. The leaves of the four-leaf-clover design had tiny ridges and cutouts that looked like the veins of actual leaves. It's weird to say that something like a key could be beautiful, but this sure was beautiful. I could imagine it sitting on a pillow behind glass in a museum.

Unfortunately, I had no way to know what it unlocked or why my real father wanted me to have it. Whatever the reason, it was the only physical proof I had that my biological parents had ever existed. I went to my desk to put it into a drawer so Mom and Dad wouldn't find it. They'd probably think I'd stolen it. I was about to drop it when I felt an odd sensation.

The key had grown warm . . . far warmer than my hand would have made it.

When the same thing happened on the roof in New York, I thought it was my imagination running wild because of the craziness that was swirling around. But now, in the quiet of my room, it felt real. The impossible thought flew into my head that it was somehow alive.

I dropped it onto my desk in case it got hot enough to burn my hand. After a few seconds I risked touching it again. It wasn't hot. It wasn't even warm.

I couldn't take it anymore. I needed to tell somebody, even if the only person around was my mother. At least she could be a witness.

I scooped it up and headed for the door . . .

. . . as the key warmed up again.

There was no mistake. I stopped and took a few steps back from the door, and the key went cold. Huh? I took a step closer to the door, and the key heated up again. I backed away, and it cooled off.

"What the heck?" I said to nobody.

I experimented a few more times. When I raised the key toward the door, it warmed up. When I pulled it away, it cooled off. This was no illusion. It was physical evidence that something weird was happening.

I cautiously walked to the door while holding the key out to see how hot it would get. I got it to within a few inches of the door when something even more impossible happened. A black spot appeared on the door's surface, just below the knob. It was as if the wood were burning. But the key wasn't hot enough to burn anything. I pulled it away quickly, and the mark disappeared.

I cautiously raised the key again. The burn mark returned, growing from a center point until it became a solid, perfect circle about an inch across. I kept moving the key closer until it almost touched the center of the mark. The "burn" continued to change. It looked as though the wood had turned molten. But wood didn't melt. Wood burned. Right? Not this wood. The dark circle seemed to go liquid and continued to move and swirl until it formed a hole.

A keyhole.

The burn mark had transformed into a perfect keyhole with a fancy, circular brass plate around it.

I pulled the key away in surprise.

The keyhole and the round brass plate disappeared.

"Oh jeez," I said, gasping.

My heart raced. Sweat from my forehead dripped into my eyes.

Was this a dream?

I lifted the key again. The brass circle with the keyhole magically returned. It was an old-fashioned keyhole, the kind that takes an old-fashioned key.

I happened to be holding an old-fashioned key.

I pushed the key forward and tentatively inserted the intricate blade into the hole.

Yeah, it fit. Perfectly. I grasped the head and twisted. I felt the tumblers of the lock inside turn easily. But that was impossible. There was no lock in this door. I continued turning the key until I heard the definite *click* of a lock being released. At the same time, the door popped open a crack.

"It's another illusion," I said to myself.

I had had enough. I yanked the door open and ran out of the room.

"Mom!" I screamed.

But I wasn't in the hallway.

Instead of leaving my room and entering the upstairs hallway of my house, I was in a room that looked like a library. Old-school wooden shelves filled with thousands of books formed long aisles that stretched into the darkness of forever.

I took a few cautious steps inside, staring in wonder at the world that I felt certain my brain had created.

Slam!

The door banged shut behind me.

I spun quickly to see an old man standing between me and the exit.

In one arm he clutched a stack of books.

In the other he held up the key he had pulled out of the lock.

"Never lose track of this, lad," he said sternly. "Unless you don't mind being lost forever."

CHAPTER
9

The old man tossed the key to me as he looked me up and down, checking me out.

"Close your mouth," he said curtly. "You look like a stupefied trout."

I snapped my mouth shut.

The guy was short and chubby and had to be at least seventy years old. He was mostly bald but had a horseshoe of snow-white hair that wrapped around the back of his head from ear to ear. He even had big, bushy sideburns that spread halfway down his cheeks. He wore wire-rimmed glasses, and if only he'd had a white beard and a sack of toys, he could have passed for Saint Nick. He didn't seem all that jolly, though. Rather than a red suit, he wore gray tweedy pants with a vest to match and a white shirt that was rolled up at the sleeves.

"Better," he said. "Have to say, you're a wee bit younger than I expected."

He spoke with the slightest hint of an Irish accent.

"How did . . . how did I . . . ?" I whispered, barely able to get the words out because my mouth was as numb as my brain.

"What're you trying to say, boy-o?" the guy snapped. "How'd you get here?"

I nodded quickly.

"The Paradox key brought you here, of course."

"The what?"

He pointed to the key in my hand.

"The Paradox key. Works on any door. Always brings you right here."

"What is *here*?" I asked, looking around at the deep aisles lined with old books.

"What does it look like?" he asked impatiently. "It's a library. I call it . . ." He paused for dramatic effect. "The Library."

He looked to me for a reaction.

I didn't give him one.

He sniffed and said, "Fine. Not exactly original, but it fits."

I held up the key and gazed at it with newfound wonder.

"So any door I use this on will magically bring me into a library?" I asked, as stupefied as the trout he had mentioned.

"Not any library. *This* library. I need to put these down; me arms are screaming."

He hurried past me toward a wooden table that sat at the end of one long aisle of bookshelves. He dumped the stack and caught his breath.

"Who are you?" I asked.

"Ain't that obvious?"

"There's nothing obvious about this place except for the name you gave it."

"I'm the librarian. Everett's the name. I'm guessing you're Marcus O'Mara."

"Wha—? How do you know me?" I asked, upshifting into the next gear of confusion.

The old man, Everett, broke out in a mischievous grin. "You learn all sorts of things in the Library. Let me show you around."

Everett walked off but stopped when he realized I wasn't following.

"Nothing to be afraid of here, Marcus. You can leave anytime you want."

"Nothing to be afraid of?" I said, incredulous. "I just

stuck a key into my bedroom door and got transported to another place. That's a little bit scary."

Everett chuckled. "S'pose so. I forget that coming here for the first time can be a tad . . . unsettling."

"That's one word for it. I can think of a few more. Have I gone crazy?"

"I'm not one to judge. But this library is as real as rain, so if you're a wee bit mad, it's got nothing to do with this place."

"I think I'm going to leave now," I said, backing toward the door.

"Ain't you the least bit curious about where you've landed?" he asked.

Truth was, I was hugely curious. Besides, if this was a dream, the old guy couldn't hurt me. Right?

"I am," I said tentatively.

"Now we're talkin'!" he said enthusiastically, and motioned for me to follow him.

I took a quick look back at the door to judge exactly where to go in case I had to make a quick getaway. It was an old-fashioned, heavy wooden door, as opposed to my normal, modern bedroom door. I sure hoped my house was on the other side of it. I clutched the key and followed the old man.

The Library looked like something out of the nineteenth century. There was a musty smell, as if the books had been there a very long time. The shelves were wooden, and the lights hanging from the ceiling were gas-burning flames.

"Did I go back in time?" I asked.

"Time has little meaning here," Everett replied.

That wasn't the answer I wanted. It only made the place feel eerier.

He walked behind a long, highly polished wooden counter that was probably the circulation desk. There were several stacks of old books on top. As Everett talked, he checked the title page of each book and divided them into piles.

"The collection is divided in two," he explained. "No Dewey Decimal system here."

He gestured to my right, where several aisles of books stretched deep into the darkness. There had to be multiple thousands of volumes, all with red, black, or brown leather bindings. None had the colorful paper jackets that you see on modern books. They looked as though they belonged in some stuffy old library where Charles Dickens hung out.

"Those volumes are all complete," he explained. "Every one of 'em has an ending."

"Don't all books have endings?" I asked.

"Not all," he said, and gestured to the aisles on my

left. There were fewer books on that side, but there still had to be thousands.

"The stories contained in those volumes have yet to be completed."

"You mean they're, like, cliff-hangers?" I asked.

"Some," he replied as he continued sorting his books. "But they weren't intended as such. These stories were all meant to be finished, and someday they will be."

"Why would you put unfinished books in a library?"

"Because the stories in 'em haven't played out yet," he explained as he gestured for me to follow him down one of the aisles of unfinished books.

I looked at the rows of books with renewed wonder.

"You mean they're not made up?" I asked.

"Not a one. All these stories actually happened. Some are *still* happening."

"But if there's no ending, why did somebody write them?"

Everett looked back at me and winked.

"Because stories need to be finished," he said, and walked on.

My brain was hurting.

"Your answers don't make sense."

"Aye, that's the crux of it," Everett said. "These stories don't make sense. That's exactly why they're here."

"Still not understanding," I said, getting frustrated.

"Follow this, lad. There are forces at work in this world that we know little about. Situations come up all the time that defy the normal rules of science and nature. Strange things. Oddities. Unexplainable phenomena. The people whose stories are in these books have found themselves in situations like that. Sound like anybody you know?"

"Well . . . yeah. I've been dealing with some strange stuff lately."

"Indeed you have."

Everett walked to the end of an aisle where there was a wooden podium with a single book on it.

"When there's a chance of finishing a story, the book gets put right here." He put his hand on the book and said, "I know what's been happening to you, Marcus. I know you were being haunted and how you got the Paradox key."

"How?" I asked, stunned.

"Because I read the book, of course," he said, as if it were the most obvious thing in the world. He picked the book up, flipped to the last page, and read:

"NEVER, EVER COME UP here again, do you understand?" Lillian Swenor scolded.

"I won't have to," her son, Alec, replied. "I gave the key to Marcus. I think it's where it belongs now."

The two looked to Marcus O'Mara, who stood over them, trying to catch his breath. He lifted up the Paradox key and held it in his open hand.

"I don't know what that key is," Mrs. Swenor said, "or why it's so important. But your father wanted Michael to give it to you, so it's yours now."

"Thank you," Marcus said.

"Promise me one thing?" Mrs. Swenor asked.

"What's that?"

"Be very, very careful."

Michael Swenor had delivered the key as he promised his best friend he would. The Paradox key was finally where it belonged.

Everett looked up at Marcus and said, "Sound familiar?"

"How is that possible?" I exclaimed while sparks flew through my brain. "It happened just a couple of hours ago."

"I told you, time has little meaning here."

Everett glanced down at the open book and said, "This was Michael Swenor's story. Now that it's complete, this book can go to the other side of the Library and . . ."

His voice trailed off as his expression grew dark. He flipped over the last page of the book, then flipped it back again, as if searching for something.

"What's the matter?" I asked.

"I don't quite know," he said, his eyebrows pinched with concern. "I've been following this story. I thought for sure it would end once you were given the Paradox key. But I'm not seeing the two most important words."

"What words are those?" I asked.

"*The end*. That's what we're always working toward here. *The end*." He snapped the book shut and added, "Oh well, so much for my powers of prediction. Seems as though Michael Swenor's story isn't quite done yet."

He placed the book back on the podium.

"So what does that mean?" I asked.

"It means your days of being haunted aren't done either," he said. "Sorry."

I backed away from the old man and banged into a shelf of books, knocking several onto the floor.

"No, I don't want anything to do with this!" I shouted at him.

"I'm afraid you don't have a choice, Marcus," Everett said with a shrug. "There's more to Michael's story, that's for certain. What we don't know is how much more."

"Yeah, we do," I said. "I know exactly how it ends.

Marcus O'Mara leaves the story, you get the key, and Michael Swenor gets to rest in peace, never to bother anybody ever again. Especially me. The end."

I threw the key at him, and he caught it awkwardly.

"You can't make up an ending," Everett said. "This ain't fiction. It has to play out for real."

"Says you," I shot back.

When I got to the door, I grabbed the knob but hesitated for one long second, fearing that when I opened the door, I'd be stepping into the nineteenth century and would get run over by a horse and buggy or something. I closed my eyes and pulled the door open to see . . .

. . . my bedroom.

"Yes!"

I jumped through and slammed the door behind me.

"Marcus!" Mom yelled from the other side. "Please open the door."

I immediately pulled the same door open again to see . . .

. . . my mom standing there in the hallway. My hallway. The Library was gone.

I was totally confused. I must have been in that library for at least fifteen minutes, but there was my mom, standing at my door, peeved, as if we were still in the middle of the argument we were having when I first got home.

"We need to talk," she said, obviously upset. "We can't sweep this under the rug."

Was it true? Did time have no meaning in that library? In "the Library"?

It took everything I had to pull my head together and focus on my mother.

"Uh, yeah. You're right. Absolutely. Just not now, okay? I'm not, uh, I'm not feeling so hot."

"Fine," she said with a resigned sigh, and backed away. "But we can't let this go."

"We won't," I said, and closed the door.

I thought for a second, then yanked it open again to see . . .

. . . the hallway. I closed the door again, then quickly reopened it to make sure. All was back to normal. I closed the door for the final time and backed into my room. I was shaking, probably from nerves or adrenaline or maybe just plain fear. What had happened? I wanted to tell myself that it was my imagination, or that I had been given some kind of hallucination-causing drug. As unlikely as either of those explanations was, they made more sense than a key that could open any door into a mysterious library full of unfinished paranormal stories.

I decided then and there that I'd never set foot in that place again. It didn't matter that I was the star of some cosmically written, unfinished drama. Mine was one story that would never be finished.

Besides, I had no way of getting back there. I had thrown the key at Everett. Maybe that was the end of Michael Swenor's story. Once I gave up the key, the tale was complete, and I could live happily ever after, ghost-free. Yeah, that sounded good.

I went to my bed and plopped down hard. All I wanted to do was sleep and maybe have a dream that made sense, like realizing I was at school wearing only underwear, or having to take a test I never studied for. I didn't even bother putting on my pajamas. I just rolled over onto my side, ready to welcome the Sandman . . .

. . . and found myself staring square at the Paradox key.

It lay on my pillow, inches from my nose.

It was mine, whether I liked it or not.

And, whether I liked it or not, it looked as though my part in this story wasn't done.

Lu and Theo stared at me with wide eyes and open mouths, as if I had just revealed to them that I was planning to grow a second head. Or maybe that would have been more believable than the story I had spun about a magical key, ghostly hauntings, and a library filled with unfinished stories.

"Well," Lu finally said, "that's something you don't hear every day."

"Can I see it?" Theo asked, his voice sounding raspy, as if he hadn't swallowed the whole time I was talking.

We were huddled on the far side of the cafeteria during a packed lunchtime.

I had the key on the leather cord around my neck, under my shirt, letting it dangle like a big old pendant necklace. I pulled it out and held it up for them to examine.

"It's pretty," Lu said. "You should polish it."

"I thought about that," I replied. "But with my luck a genie would show up."

"It's old," Theo said, shifting into analytical mode. "Well over a hundred years. They don't make keys like this anymore."

"And how would you know that?" Lu asked skeptically.

"Because I'm smart" was Theo's simple, typical answer.

"What do you guys think?" I asked while tucking the key back under my shirt. "Easy answer is I'm crazy, but I don't feel crazy. After that, I've got nothing."

"All righty," Theo said while squeezing his earlobe. "There could be a few explanations. We talked about stress. People can imagine all sorts of things while under duress."

"That goes back to being crazy," I said. "Next."

"You mentioned hallucinogens. There are some powerful drugs that could cause you to see things, but why would anybody do that to you?"

"And I feel fine," I said. "It's not like I'm loopy or anything."

"Then I suppose there's the possibility that someone's

playing an elaborate prank," Theo said. "But, given what you've told us, *elaborate* would be an understatement."

"That leaves just one possibility," Lu said.

"Please, tell me!" I exclaimed.

She scratched her neck nervously and said, "It could all be true."

I jumped out of my chair, then sat back down again. Then stood up. The nervous energy was hard to control.

"Do you know what that means?" I said. "All the stuff we see in movies and read in books, all the ghost stories and magical stuff and weird, unexplainable craziness, would be possible. That changes . . . everything!"

"No, it doesn't," Lu argued. "All it means is sometimes things happen that we can't explain."

"Everything can be explained," Theo said with authority.

"Okay, sure," Lu shot back at him. "The explanation is, it can't be explained. It's like psychic people or people who have memories of past lives. There's no scientific explanation for those things, but they're real."

"There are most definitely explanations," Theo said stubbornly. "They're hoaxes."

"Could you just try to open your narrow mind for once?" Lu snapped. "Not everything can be calculated scientifically."

"Yes, it can," Theo replied with total conviction.

"Then how do you explain what's happening to Marcus?" she asked, folding her arms.

Theo started to answer quickly but stopped himself.

"I can't," he admitted. "But I will. If there's one thing I'm completely certain of, it's that there is nothing supernatural going on here. There's no such thing as ghosts. Or curses. Or magical libraries. That's just not how the world works. When you're all willing to discuss this logically, I'm available."

He picked up his books and his lunch tray and stormed off.

"Why's he so bent?" I asked. "He's not the one hallucinating."

"He doesn't like it when his orderly world turns out to be not so orderly," Lu said.

"I don't like it much either."

"Maybe you should tell your parents."

"No," I said quickly. "They're the last people I want to tell."

"Why?"

I didn't answer right away. I'd never shared my feelings about my parents with anybody.

"What's going on with you and your folks, Marcus?" Lu asked.

"They wish they hadn't adopted me."

"What? No! Why do you say that?"

"Because they wanted a certain kind of kid . . . and I'm not it. My mother even said so."

"She did not."

"Yeah, she kind of did. It's not like it was a surprise. They spend a whole lot of time telling me about all the things I do wrong and how disappointed and frustrated they are. It gets old, you know?"

"All parents do that," Lu said. "My mom hates that I play roller derby. She wants me to be a cheerleader. Can you see that? I don't do pep."

"This is different. They're angry all the time, and the more we talk about it, the worse it gets. I'm not saying I'm perfect, but I know they wish they'd adopted somebody else. To be honest, sometimes I wish that too."

"Don't say that."

"At least one good thing came from this key. I got to learn a little about my real parents."

The bell rang, and kids immediately started flooding out of the cafeteria.

Lu and I didn't move as kids hurried past.

"I don't know about this library thing," Lu said, "but the one thing I do know is that your real parents are the people you're living with right now."

I grabbed my books and stood up. "Here's something *I* know. I'm never putting this key anywhere near a door again."

Lu reached forward, stuck out her finger, and touched the key through my shirt.

"Don't be so quick to say that," she said. "There might be all sorts of things you could learn in a library like that." She gave me a smile and said, "Just sayin'."

That afternoon I served my third day of detention. Ms. Holden was the monitor again, and this time she didn't leave me alone. That was fine by me. I welcomed the company. Or the protection. I tried to negotiate with her, saying how my day of being suspended should count against my detention, but she didn't buy it. Though I did get a smile out of her for trying.

The detention period passed without any spooky business. It gave me hope that my part in Michael Swenor's story was done after all. I didn't live far from school, so every day I walked home along the sidewalks of suburban Stony Brook. Since school had been out for an hour, all the buses and frantic moms in SUVs were long gone. The street in front of the building was deserted. It was so quiet I didn't bother walking to the corner to cross. I looked both ways to make sure all was clear, and I was about to step off the curb when I looked to the far side—to see that the street wasn't empty after all.

Standing on the sidewalk directly across the street from me was Michael Swenor.

No mistake. It was him. The pajamas and bathrobe were gone. He looked just as he did in the newspaper picture, wearing a dark firefighter's uniform. He stood there alone, looking straight at me with an eerily blank expression.

My brain locked. I was staring at a ghost, and the ghost was staring back. What did he want?

The guy slowly raised his arm. I thought he was going to wave at me, but instead he held the palm of his hand toward me in a *stop* gesture, as if telling me not to move.

No problem. I didn't want to go anywhere near him.

A second later, a large pink rubber ball bounced past me from behind and rolled into the street. My first impulse was to run after it, but I didn't. I was still in shock.

A little girl ran past me from behind. She had long red hair that fell over her shoulders, and she wore a cute little-girl pink party dress. She bounded right into the street without a care, chasing after the ball.

"Hey, careful!" I shouted.

A car came screaming around the corner. It turned so quickly that its wheels squealed on the pavement. It straightened out and accelerated . . . headed right for the little girl.

Instinct took over. I ran into the street, scooped the girl up, and kept running. It wasn't a very close call, but my heart was beating like crazy just the same. The car sped past, filled with high school guys hanging out the windows.

"Get out of the road, idiot!" one shouted as they flew past.

"Slow down!" I yelled after them.

They didn't, and sped off.

"You gotta be careful," I said to the girl as I put her down on the far sidewalk. "Where's your mother?"

The girl looked up at me, and my knees buckled.

Her face wasn't real. It was a plastic doll's face, framed by long red hair. But it wasn't just any doll's face. It was the face of the old woman. Her wild eyes looked right at me as the doll's hinged mouth moved to speak.

"Surrender the key," she said in the gnarly voice of the old lady, "or more will die."

I took a few quick steps back as if I'd been pushed. The girl, or the doll or the old lady or whatever it was, turned and skipped away down the sidewalk. I stood there watching, stunned, as it rounded a corner and was gone.

I didn't move for a solid ten seconds, trying to unfreeze my brain. Finally, I remembered.

Michael Swenor.

I spun toward the spot where the ghost had been standing.

He was gone. The entire block was deserted. Nobody saw what had happened but me.

Why had he come back? What did he want? Was he trying to stop me from going into the road to save . . . who? The old witch? Was he protecting me?

I had to will my feet to move. I sprinted along the sidewalk, barely looking for cars as I crossed multiple streets, and didn't stop moving until I got home. I slammed the door and stood in our foyer, gasping for breath. I needed water, so I hurried into the kitchen and grabbed a glass, then changed my mind and put my head directly under the faucet.

As I gulped down the water, my eye caught something on the counter. It was a plate filled with brownies. My favorite. Dark-chocolate Ghirardelli. Next to it was a note. It was a folded piece of paper with my name on it. I didn't want to look at it. I thought for sure it would say *Surrender the key*. Three words I had grown to hate.

Only now there were more words to worry about: *Or more will die*.

That was what the old lady–girl doll–witch had said.

Or more will die.

I summoned my courage, grabbed the note, and read.

It was from Mom. I recognized her perfect penmanship.

Let's talk when I get home. I made your favorite brownies. Don't eat them all. Oh, never mind, eat them all if you want. Mom.

Was this note really from Mom? Or was it another illusion to try to get me to eat a plate of poisoned brownies? It sure didn't sound like Mom. I wanted to believe that she was reaching out to try to make things right, but I wasn't sure what I could believe anymore.

Or more will die.

That wasn't a threat against me. It was a warning. Was the old witch going after people I cared about? There was only one thing I knew for sure: my role in Michael Swenor's story was not finished.

Not by a long shot.

I left without grabbing a brownie. I didn't want to take the chance. I went upstairs to my room, threw my books down on my desk, and pulled the key out from under my shirt. How could I surrender it? If I gave it up, I'd lose the one connection I had to my real parents, but if it meant ending the haunting and protecting others from this crazy old lady, how could I keep it?

I walked to my bedroom door and felt the key grow warm in my hand, as if it was telling me what to do. I held it out toward the door. Instantly, the dark spot returned and transformed into the brass keyhole.

Message received.

I inserted the key into the lock, twisted it, and opened the door to return to the Library.

CHAPTER
11

The place was as quiet as—well, as a library.

My footsteps echoed back at me as I walked slowly past the long corridors of books. I didn't call out to announce that I was back. That would have felt wrong. After all, it was a library. Instead, I listened for signs of life.

The ancient room was suddenly feeling less like a library and more like a tomb. It didn't help knowing that all the books were filled with true stories about ghosts and other assorted oddities. I took a few more steps and heard the faint sound of rustling pages. Quickly, I headed in that direction. After passing a few more aisles of endless bookcases, I arrived at the circulation desk, where Everett was sitting on a high stool, reading. His wire-rim spectacles were down on the end of his nose as he squinted in concentration at a book that was open in front of him. I stood a few yards away, hoping he would notice me.

After a few awkward seconds, I cleared my throat.

He didn't look up.

"I'm back," I said sheepishly.

"Obviously," Everett said without looking at me.

"You were right," I said. "Michael Swenor's story isn't done, and I'm still part of it. I want to know how I can finish it."

That got his attention. He looked up at me over the top of his glasses.

"What changed your mind?" he asked. "Perhaps it was the odd young lass who was nearly run down by the car? Brave rescue, by the way. Quick thinking. Good instincts."

Once again my knees went weak.

"How do you know about that?" I asked, incredulous.

Everett spun the book around and tapped the page. I looked down at the printed words to read:

THE LITTLE GIRL HAD the face of a wizened old doll with wild eyes. She fixed her intense gaze on Marcus and said, "Surrender the key, or more will die."

"Or more will die," Everett said, raising his eyebrows. "Sounds a bit ominous."

"Who wrote this?" I demanded. "Nobody else was there."

"Eyes are everywhere," Everett said. "Especially when there's a disruption."

"Disruption?"

"That's what I call it. Like I told you before, the course of human events doesn't always follow the rules of science and nature. There are forces at work that can't be explained. That's what this library is about. We document, investigate, and try to put things right."

"Who's *we*?"

Everett stared me straight in the eye. I felt as though he was trying to read my mind. Or maybe he was deciding if I could handle the answer I was asking for. He took off his glasses and wiped them with a rumpled handkerchief he pulled from his back pocket.

"I'm going to ask you a question," he said. "Your answer will either make this a far sight easier or cause a boatload of grief for the both of us."

"Go for it."

"Do you believe in ghosts?"

He kept his eyes on me with an intensity that meant he was dead serious.

Did I believe in ghosts? Good question.

"If you'd asked me that a couple of days ago, I would have thought you were the one who was crazy," I said.

"And now?"

"Yeah, I believe in ghosts. Though I'm not sure that's better than being crazy."

Everett gave a satisfied nod as he slipped his glasses into his vest pocket. "It is. It means you've accepted reality."

"Reality?" I said, scoffing. "I don't know what that is anymore."

Everett closed the book, stood up, and gestured for me to follow. He rounded the counter and waddled down one of the long aisles, walking with a slight limp that proved he was every bit as old as he looked.

"There is a natural order to life, Marcus," he said. "It's why the world exists and keeps spinning. But every so often the balance gets thrown off. People do things they shouldn't. Or something unexpected happens that knocks somebody's train off the tracks. That's when things become unsettled. Unfinished."

"Disrupted."

"Aye! Good. That's where we come in. We try to make things right."

He scanned the rows of books.

"Here's a perfect example," he said with enthusiasm as he pulled an ancient volume off the shelf. "A classic.

The fella in this story was poisoned by his business partner. Clear case of greed. The killer got off scot-free. There's the disruption. The victim was wronged, and his spirit couldn't rest in peace till justice was served. Thanks to an agent from the Library, the truth came out. That's what I call the folks who finish the stories. Agents. This lass revealed the identity of the murderer with help from the victim himself. Or his spirit. She finished the story, and the spirit was able to move on. These shelves are packed with stories like that. I file 'em under *Justice*."

"How did the agent finish the story?" I asked. "Did she, like, do research?"

"You could say that. Firsthand research. When an agent leaves the Library with one of these books, they step into its story. They become part of it."

"Wait, what? For real?"

"Aye. How else can they put things right?"

"That's impossible," I said.

"You thought ghosts were impossible until a few days ago, didn't ya?" he said, and shoved the book into my hands. "Here's another good one," he said as he pulled down a book with a black binding. "Happened in New Orleans. Family with three young ones. One morning all three tykes woke up mute. Just like that. Couldn't say a word, not even a whisper. Turned out the elderly woman who lived in the apartment below fancied herself to be a voodoo queen. The wee ones had been making too much noise for her liking, disturbing her afternoon naps. She used her dark magic to cast a spell that kept 'em quiet. Doctors couldn't figure out what was wrong with 'em, but we did."

"So the agent was transported to New Orleans and figured this out?" I asked.

"Aye. I shelve that one under *Curses*."

He handed me the book.

I stared at it, trying to understand the magic that could send a living, breathing person to another place.

"So these unfinished stories are all happening right now?" I asked.

"Some are. Like Michael Swenor's story. But not all stories are happening today. Many of these tales go a ways back, but that doesn't stop us from trying to finish 'em up."

"Seriously? The Library is like a time machine?"

"I told you, time doesn't mean much here."

I was reeling. The more I learned about this oddball library, the wilder it all seemed.

"Who writes the stories?" I asked.

"Spirits, of course," Everett said casually. "Like I said, eyes are everywhere."

He must have seen the stunned expression on my

face, because he gave me an innocent shrug and said, "Why so surprised? You said you believed."

He turned away and headed back toward the circulation desk.

I jammed the books back onto the shelf and hurried after him.

"You're telling me ghosts are roaming everywhere, taking notes on strange happenings and writing books about them?"

"More or less," he replied.

"I'm never going to the bathroom again."

Everett frowned and said, "Please, boy-o. There are limits."

"So a spirit was watching what happened with me and the little girl and wrote it all down?"

Everett picked up the book he'd been reading from and held it up. "Every last detail. But that's not always the case. They don't catch everything. We have to fill in the blanks ourselves. That's our job."

"Then if the spirits are everywhere, why don't they help out? They could have saved Michael Swenor from falling off that roof."

"Doesn't work like that. Spirits can't affect events, only observe them. That's why we need the living agents."

"What about you? You read all the books. You

knew what was going on. Why didn't you help Michael Swenor?"

"I told you, spirits can't affect events."

"But you're not—"

The full meaning of his answer took a few seconds to sink in.

"Wait. That means . . ."

Everett winked at me and said, "Boo."

I backed away so fast I slammed into a bookcase.

"You're dead?" I said, my voice cracking.

"Easy now—you look like you've seen a ghost. Oh, wait . . ."

He wheezed out a laugh, as if pleased by his own cleverness.

I wanted to run the heck out of there, but the memory of that old witch's face came back to me. She was way more frightening than this guy. Even if he was a ghost.

"Why am I here?" I asked, trying to keep my voice from rising three octaves. "Why did my father have this key? And who is that old lady?"

"Answers to the first two questions are easy," Everett said. "Your father was an agent of the Library. Seems as though he wants you to follow in his footsteps."

"You mean my real father? My biological father?"

"Yes. Good man, Jim Roxbury. He often brought along a young buddy to help him out. Michael Swenor."

"Michael Swenor came here? You knew him?"

"Aye. Smart fella. Good agent. Really cared. Open that drawer in front of you there. He left something here a while back."

I looked down at the desk to see several drawers with brass handles. I pulled out the drawer directly in front of me and saw that it contained a single item. It was a badge. A silver New York City firefighter's badge.

"Pick it up," Everett commanded.

I reached into the drawer and retrieved the heavy silver badge, which had an engine company number as well as the number of the firefighter.

"This was Michael Swenor's?" I asked.

"Aye. Such a good man. Just like your father."

Another piece of the puzzle clicked into place. Mrs. Swenor told me that her husband investigated paranormal occurrences but never left the apartment. Turns out he left the apartment plenty. He came to the Library, and since time didn't matter here, when he returned home, no time had passed. It was as though he had never left home.

"It pains me that he passed the way he did," Everett said.

I moved to put the badge back in the drawer.

He stopped me. "Take it. That badge is from the mortal world. It shouldn't be here."

"What am I supposed to do with it?"

"Whatever you'd like."

I slipped the heavy metal badge into the pocket of my hoodie.

"Now," Everett went on, "it's the answer to your third question that has me worried."

He sat back down behind the counter and opened the book again.

"The thing about these stories is that they only tell us what happened. They don't predict the future."

"Does it say who the old lady is?" I asked.

Everett took a worried breath and said, "I'm afraid so. She may be old, but she is by no means a lady."

"She's a man?" I asked, incredulous.

"Let's call it a . . . thing. That's as good a word as any. That thing has been the subject of many of the stories we've got here in the Library, which is why I suspect it wants the key. It doesn't want any of the stories to be finished."

"Why not?" I asked.

Everett slid the book over to me and said one word. "Read."

The pages were yellowed, as if the book had been printed a long time ago. Printed? Is that what spirit authors did? Was there some magical laser printer that spit these books out? I flipped to the first page and read:

THE PHANTOM GOES BY many names: *El Coco, Nøkken, Mörkö, Babau,* and *the Boggin.* There are countless others, depending on the country and culture that share the tales. Though it is a creature whose myth has grown, its actual origin can be traced back to the time of the druids. Ancient texts relate how a powerful specter was conjured by mystics as a means to control disobedient children. Its entire reason for being was to use fear as a tool to discipline defiant young ones.

However, the power of the phantom proved to be more of a problem than a solution. Its mindless craving to create fear only grew stronger as it spread terror by reaching into the minds of its young victims to show them the images and apparitions they feared most. Word of this frightening spirit spread throughout the ancient world, prompting the creation of stories and legends that continue to grow, even in modern times. Though most of the stories are myth, the monster itself is very real.

The ancients had no way of destroying it, but in its creation they anticipated a way to entrap and control it. Through the centuries it has been imprisoned many times, only to find its way loose to continue its insatiable quest to spread fear and terror.

I pushed the book away and looked to Everett, who was leaning back in his chair with his hands folded over his round belly.

"You're kidding me, right?" I asked.

"Is there a problem?"

"Yeah, there's a problem. You know what this is saying, don't you?"

"I have a pretty good idea."

"Me too," I shot back nervously. "This says the legend is true."

"That's pretty much how I see it."

"But that's just—crazy," I said as my heart raced. "It's a fairy tale. A myth. Like Frankenstein. Or Dracula. It's a . . . a . . . joke."

"Joke? Has anything you've seen come across as remotely funny?"

"But it's a fictional character."

"Tell that to Michael Swenor the next time you see him."

I slammed the book shut and backed away.

"I don't believe it."

"What don't you believe, Marcus? That these stories are real? That I'm a spirit? That this library is full of actual stories about people who need our help? Or that what you just read is true?"

My mind was spinning. After all I'd seen, all I'd

been through, this was the most impossible thing to accept.

"I—I don't know," I stammered.

"Well, get your head around it, boy-o," Everett said, turning serious. "You've seen the illusions. You've felt the fear. I don't know exactly how Michael Swenor ties in to it, but from what I can see, that thing is on the loose again, and it's set its sights on the Library. It tried to stop you from getting the Paradox key, but now that you've got it, it's coming after you. With that key, it could destroy this place and the work we've been doing here for eons. That's what it wants, Marcus. It wants to destroy the Library, and it'll stop anyone who gets in its way. Like Michael Swenor . . . and now you."

I looked to the book that sat between us on the counter. It contained a story. An impossible story. Yet I knew it was true, because I'd seen it in action.

"So it isn't a myth," I said soberly. "There really is a boogeyman."

"Aye," Everett said.

"I . . . I gotta think," I said, backing away. "I'm going home."

"Take this with you," he said, and held out the book that contained Michael Swenor's story.

I didn't take it. It was kryptonite. I backed away farther, nearly tripping on the edge of a bookcase.

"I don't want it," I said.

Everett shrugged and put the book on the podium. "No matter. You don't really need it. You're already in the story."

"That's not making me feel better."

"You've got a lot to chew over," Everett said. "But understand, you're part of this. You know it, and the Boggin knows it. Question is, what're you going to do about it?"

I couldn't get out of there fast enough and hurried for the door.

"Keep your wits about you, son," Everett called out. "Or more will die."

I threw the door open and jumped through into . . .

. . . my bedroom.

Phew.

"Marcus?" my mother called from downstairs. "Are you home?"

Good question. Was I home? Or out of my mind? I reopened the door to see . . . our hallway. Without the key in the magical lock, the door didn't open back into the Library.

"Marcus?"

"Yeah?" I called out.

"Come down!"

I wasn't in the mood to have another duel with my mother. Then again, she'd baked me brownies. Maybe there was a truce in effect. I had to shake away the thoughts of what I'd just heard from Everett and get my head together enough to act normal. I slipped Michael Swenor's badge out of my hoodie and dropped it into my desk drawer. I rubbed my face, stuck the key under my shirt, and headed downstairs.

Mom was waiting at the foot of the stairs with a big smile. Good start.

"What's up?" I asked, trying to sound all casual, as if nothing at all were up.

"I want to introduce you to someone," she said, and led me toward the living room. "She's thinking of moving into the area and wanted to meet some of the neighbors."

I couldn't have cared less about a new neighbor, but in order to keep the peace, I went along. I was going to have to put on my "polite to adults" face and pretend I cared.

Mom led me down the hall, into the living room.

"Marcus," she said, "this is Miss Bogg."

A woman was sitting in our high-backed easy chair with her back to me. When we entered she stood up and turned to face me . . .

. . . and I nearly passed out.

It was the old lady.

The Boggin. El Coco. Babau. Whatever.

The boogeyman was a woman, and she was in our house.

"Hello, young man," she said in the voice of a kindly old grandma. "So nice to meet you."

CHAPTER
12

I stood there staring at the old lady, or whatever she was, with my mouth hanging open.

Mom tried to make nice. "You two talk, and I'll get us something to nibble on."

"Please, don't go to any trouble for me," the beastly old lady said so sweetly it almost made me believe she was human.

Almost.

"No trouble," Mom said over her shoulder as she hurried out. "Make yourself at home. Marcus, be a good host."

I didn't want to be a host, good or otherwise, and I definitely didn't want her making herself at home. I

wanted this thing gone. As soon as my mother left the room, the old lady turned her crazy gaze on me.

"Hello, Marcus," she said, way too nicely.

I think my blood froze in my veins.

"What do you want?" I asked, trying to keep my voice from quivering.

"You know very well," she replied kindly, but with a hint of acid that made my skin crawl.

I backed away, as if being a few feet farther from her would make her less dangerous. It was hard to look into her wild eyes. It was like staring straight into the double barrels of a shotgun.

"You killed Michael Swenor," I said.

She shrugged casually, as if I had said it looked like rain.

"He did not do what I asked," she said dismissively. "Such a simple request. I wanted the key. Instead, it was passed to you."

I felt the weight of the heavy brass key hanging around my neck.

"Why do you want it so bad, anyway?" I asked. "So you can destroy the Library?"

The old lady stiffened as if a simple mention of the Library gave her the chills. How odd is that? The boogeyman was afraid of something.

Note to self . . .

"You defy me?" she said indignantly. "Me? The very essence of fear? For centuries children have been assured I'm a myth, but in the dark corners of their imaginations, they know that I am oh so very real. I'm always out there, perched on the edge of their dreams. Watching and waiting. And now I'm here. With you."

She stalked toward me slowly. I backed off, trying not to knock over any tables or lamps.

"But you're not real," I said. "You weren't born. You were conjured."

"With only one purpose."

"No. Not only one purpose. You don't just frighten people. You killed Michael Swenor."

"He was a threat. The Library is a threat. Its agents know my truth and continually try to contain me. Can you blame me for fighting back? They will not give up unless I stop them. For that, I need the key."

I wanted to rip the key from around my neck and throw it at her. If she wanted the Library spirits to leave her alone, why should I care? I wanted nothing to do with Everett and that creepy old place.

I was a second away from giving her the stupid key and ending this nightmare when I remembered why it was given to me.

My father wanted me to have it.

My real father.

He had been an agent of the Library. I didn't think for a second that I would be able to do the same, but my father wanted me to try. That was why I was standing face to face with a spirit who had the power to terrify and, at the moment, was doing a pretty decent job of it.

"What happens if I don't give it to you?" I asked nervously. "You going to kill me like you killed Michael Swenor and just take it?"

The demon who called herself Miss Bogg stopped walking. We were only a few feet apart.

She had no comeback.

That was when I knew.

"Surrender the key," I said. "You can't take it, can you? I have to give it up."

The woman held out a gnarled, wrinkly hand that had long, yellowed, clawlike nails.

"Give it to me," she demanded with a hint of frustration.

"Sorry," I said defiantly. "No chance."

She stared at me for several seconds. I braced myself against . . . what? Was she going to reach into my brain and create another illusion to threaten me?

"You are correct," she said with a cold smile. "The holder of the key must surrender it. As long as you possess it, you will not be harmed."

"Best news I've heard all day."

"The same does not apply to those you care about."

My stomach sank.

"Teatime!" Mom announced as she walked into the room.

She hurried over to us, holding a tray with an old-fashioned copper teapot that she brought out only on special occasions. Mom walked right up to us and held out the tray with the gleaming orange pot for Miss Bogg to admire.

"Tea brewed the old-fashioned way!" she announced proudly.

The Boggin's confident smile fell quickly, and she lurched away as if the tray were on fire. She hurried for the door faster than I'd seen any old lady move, ever. I shouldn't have been surprised, because she wasn't really an old lady.

"Miss Bogg?" Mom called out, confused.

The fiend didn't turn back. She went straight for the front door and left without saying a word.

I just stood there, dumbfounded. Mom watched with dismay, still holding the tray out. She turned to me and said, "What did you say to her?"

I immediately got defensive. It was force of habit when you were always being accused of things you didn't do.

"Me? Nothing."

"You must have said something. Why would she leave like that?"

"I'm just as surprised as you are," I said. "Maybe she's allergic to tea."

Mom's expression turned cold. "Not funny. A minute ago she was the sweetest old lady in the world, and then suddenly she couldn't get out of here fast enough. What happened while I was gone?"

What could I say? I couldn't exactly tell her the truth. *Well, Mom, the thing is, that old lady is the boogeyman. Yup. The boogeyman. Funny thing, huh? The boogeyman is really a boogeywoman! Who knew?*

That wouldn't fly.

"I swear, Mom. I didn't do anything wrong. But she was kind of creepy, to be honest. I'm glad she's gone."

"Creepy? She was the least creepy person I've ever met. Did you tell her you thought she was creepy?"

"No! I mean, not really."

"Unbelievable!" she exclaimed.

"It wasn't like that," I said, but couldn't back that up.

"Go after her and apologize," she demanded.

"No way!"

"Go! Take some responsibility. Catch her. Now!"

I opened my mouth to protest, but no words came out. I had no choice but to leave, so I hurried out the door. When I hit the walkway that led to the street, I stopped and looked around in case Miss Bogg, or whatever her real name was, was waiting to pounce on me.

The sun had just set. There were far too many deepening shadows and places for the Boggin to be lurking for me to feel safe out there. But I couldn't go back inside. At least not right away. So I jammed my hands into my pockets, put my head down, and walked quickly to the street and along the sidewalk, away from my house. I had no destination in mind. I just wanted to keep moving.

The words of the Boggin, Miss Bogg, kept running through my head. She wanted the key so she could destroy the Library, and she threatened to hurt the people I cared about if she didn't get it. What was I supposed to do? My parents wouldn't believe me. I couldn't go to the police, because they'd have me committed. I could surrender the key, but would my father, my birth father, want me to do that? It could mean the end of the Library.

I needed somebody to help me think things through.

That was when I saw Michael Swenor.

The ghost stood on the street corner a block away. I might not even have seen him except that the streetlamp had kicked on over his head, bathing the corner in light. He stood staring at me with that same haunted, blank look that totally creeped me out.

"Don't move!" I shouted, and ran for him.

He didn't listen to me. Could ghosts even hear? He

turned and walked away slowly, down the sidewalk, disappearing behind a corner hedge.

I sprinted to the corner and turned his way to see that he hadn't actually disappeared. But he was suddenly three blocks away. It was impossible for anybody except a ghost, I guess, to have moved that fast.

"Stop!" I yelled, and sprinted after him.

Swenor walked away again, slowly. I didn't think for a second that I could catch up with him, since ghosts seemed to be able to jump around at the speed of light, but I had to try. When I got to the spot where he'd last stood, I glanced around to see him only one block away, standing in the middle of the sidewalk.

"Stand still!" I called out to him as I inched forward. This time he didn't move.

"This is your story," I said. "But I don't know how to finish it. You know about the Boggin; I know you do. If I don't give it the key, it'll come after the people I care about. What am I supposed to do?"

I kept walking until I was only a few yards from him, the closest I'd gotten since the classroom where I first saw him. It was close enough to see the sad look in his eyes.

"I need help," I said as I stepped up to him. "I can't do this alone."

Swenor turned toward the house we were standing in front of, looked back to me, and disappeared. *Poof.* One second he was there and looking as solid as me; the next second there was only air.

I let out a gasp. Yes, I believed in ghosts, but I still wasn't used to seeing them pop in and out like that. What was the point? Why had he shown himself to me again? He didn't have anything to give me, and he wasn't trying to protect me. What was I missing?

I looked toward the house he had led me to and caught my breath.

He had brought me to Lu's house.

I couldn't begin to imagine why he'd done that, but I definitely needed somebody to talk to. Lu would listen.

"Marcus!" Mrs. Lu exclaimed when she opened her front door. "How the heck are you?"

Lu's parents were cool.

"I'm good. Is Lu—I mean, is Annabella home?"

"She's doing homework in her room, I hope. Or maybe she's rolling around in the basement. I can't keep track of that girl."

"Okay if I go see?"

"Sure. Just don't let her talk you into putting on skates. She'll hurt you."

I hurried into the house and ran straight up the stairs.

Mrs. Lu wasn't one of those moms who didn't let boys and girls exist in the same room alone. Like I said, she was cool.

I found Lu at her desk with her earbuds in, sketching.

"Hey," I said, loud enough for her to hear over her music.

She pulled out her earbuds, looked at me, and frowned.

"Oh man, what happened?" she asked.

"Why? Do I look that bad?"

"If I didn't know better, I'd say you hadn't slept in a week."

"That's exactly how I feel."

I sat down on the end of her bed and spent ten minutes unloading. I told her about everything: the little girl who wasn't a little girl; my visit to the Library; the reappearances of Michael Swenor, and how he'd led me to her house; and, finally, the truth about the Boggin and how it turned up at my house.

She listened without comment. I had her full attention, which wasn't easy to get from Lu.

"I'm lost," I said. "If I don't give her the key, she'll come after the people I care about. But if I give it up, she'll destroy that library, and all the people whose stories aren't finished will be left in some kind of spirit limbo."

Lu rubbed her forehead, leaving a smudge from the drawing charcoal. She looked down at her paper and absently sketched some more. She wasn't ignoring me. She was thinking.

After a few minutes she dropped the charcoal and said, "I don't know what you should do."

"That's it?" I asked, peeved. "Nothing? No thoughts? No insight? No different way of looking at things I might have missed?"

"Nope."

"Gee, thanks," I said, and got up to leave.

"Wait," she said quickly. "There's really only one person who can help."

I sat back down on the bed.

"Who?"

"That Everett guy. The librarian."

I put my hand to my chest and felt the key.

"I don't want to go back there."

"I hear you. But if this is all true, it might be a whole lot scarier if you don't."

I couldn't argue with that.

"Do you believe me?" I asked.

"I don't know. It's a lot. But I don't think you're making it up. There's only one way for me to know for sure."

"What's that?" I asked.

"Take me with you."

"No. No way. My father brought Michael Swenor to that library, and look what happened to him."

Lu was strangely silent. That wasn't like her. Something was on her mind.

"What?" I asked.

"The Library is about unfinished stories, right? Strange phenomena that can't be explained? Disruptions?"

"Yeah, so?"

"About six months ago my cousin Jenny disappeared. She's run away before. Lots of times. She gets in trouble a lot. But this time she just, like, vanished. Everyone hopes she'll turn up, like always, but the longer it goes on, the scarier it gets. Nobody says it, but we're all afraid that something really bad happened to her."

"Man, I'm sorry."

"I wonder if what happened to Jenny is, like, a . . . disruption?"

The word echoed in my head as if she had screamed it.

"You think her story might be in one of the books in the Library?" I asked.

Lu shrugged. "I don't know. Maybe. I wouldn't mind finding out."

"I don't know—"

"Look, Marcus, this Boggin thing threatened to hurt

the people you care about. We're best friends. You think you're protecting me by keeping me away? I think I'm already in trouble."

I was torn. The last thing I wanted to do was put Lu in danger.

"I'll tell you something else. I think I know why Michael Swenor led you here."

"Really? Why?"

"He knows you need help, like I'm sure your father needed help when he was an agent of the Library. They were friends. He helped your father. Now let me help you."

"But I don't want you to get hurt," I said.

"Then take me to the Library and give me a chance to protect myself. Who knows? You might be doing me a favor."

I dug under the collar of my shirt and pulled the cord from around my neck.

"If anything happens to you—"

"I can take care of myself," she said as she hurried to her desk. She grabbed her roller derby wrist guards and slipped them onto her hands. "In case I have to take a swing at somebody."

Lu was tough, but if she thought throwing a punch at somebody was going to protect us from the kind of trouble the Boggin could bring, she was dreaming.

"Good thinking," I said. Why burst her bubble?

"Then let's go," she said with excitement.

I walked to her bedroom door and felt the key grow warm in my hand. Lu stood behind me as I raised it toward the doorknob. The black spot appeared below the knob and quickly transformed into the keyhole.

"And there it goes," Lu said, stunned.

"There what goes?"

"Any doubt I had that this is real."

"Hang on, we're just getting started."

I put the key into the lock, twisted it until the tumblers clicked, and opened the door into another world.

CHAPTER
13

When we stepped into the Library, Everett was waiting for us just inside the door.

He looked upset, shifting his weight from one foot to the other impatiently. Or maybe he just had to go to the bathroom. Did ghosts use the bathroom?

"About time you came back," he said curtly. "Come with me."

He turned and headed deeper into the room. I followed for a few steps, then stopped when I remembered that Lu was visiting this supernatural room for the first time. I looked back to see that she was still standing in the doorway, totally shaken.

"You okay?" I asked.

"I said I believed you, but I didn't really believe you."

She looked around, wide-eyed, as if we'd just stepped into another dimension, which was exactly what we'd done.

"I know, it's crazy," I said. "But there's nothing to be afraid of here. I think. Can't say the same about back in real life."

Everett came charging back.

"What's the holdup?" he said as he pushed the door closed behind Lu.

I gestured to Lu. Everett focused on her and downshifted.

"Annabella Lu. Pleased to meet you, lass. I've read a lot about you. I promise, there ain't nothing in here you can't handle."

"Really?" Lu replied. "It's a supernatural library filled with unfinished ghost stories, written by ghosts, where time has no meaning, and the boogeyman wants to blow it all up. What exactly is it you think I can handle about any of that?"

"I hear ya," Everett said with sympathy. "It'll take a while for you to wrap your mind around it all. But don't worry, we'll ease you in."

He turned to walk off and then looked back with an afterthought.

"Oh, but don't forget the part about you being in mortal danger because you're a friend of Marcus's."

He gave her a quick smile and hurried away.

Lu shot me a sick look. "So much for easing me in."

"He's upset about something," I said.

"Good. That makes all of us."

"C'mon," I said, and took her hand.

I had to pull her to keep moving as she gazed around in wonder at the endless aisles of books. We found Everett behind the circulation desk with a couple of books open in front of him.

"Good news and bad news," he said. "I found a number of stories about the Boggin. Seems it's turned up throughout history, and every time it does, it causes the same kind of trouble you've been going through."

"Is that the good news or the bad news?" I asked.

"This is a completed story," he said, shoving a book toward us. "Read the part I highlighted."

Lu and I read the following to ourselves:

THE DRUIDS HAD NO idea of the extent of the horrible power they had unleashed. However, they had the foresight to create a means to restrain the spirit, in order to call upon it at times of their choosing. A vessel was created of an element that was both plentiful and readily available. It being the Bronze Age, the choice was

143

copper. This metal is the spirit's weakness. Throughout the centuries the makeup of the vessels changed, but a seal of copper ensured that the phantom would be contained. Only when the seal was broken by a mortal would the spirit be released to roam free.

"Copper," I said. "My mother offered Miss Bogg tea in a copper teakettle. The old witch jumped away like it was garlic and she was a vampire."

"That's a myth, by the way," Everett said.

We both looked to him, questioning.

"Garlic and vampires," Everett said innocently. "Not true."

"You know about vampires?" I asked.

Everett shrugged. "There are all kinds of stories in the Library."

"Seriously?" Lu said, squeamish. "Never mind, don't answer that. I don't want to know."

"That's the good news?" I asked skeptically. "We have to get her to jump into a copper teakettle?"

"Not *we*," Everett said. "*You*. I can't leave here, remember?"

"The good news isn't all that good," Lu said.

"But it is!" Everett exclaimed. "It means there's a way to stop that horrid spirit. It's all in the books. The Boggin has escaped and caused trouble more times than

I can count, but it's also been trapped just as often. That proves it can be done."

"Okay," I said. "That's good, but barely. What's the bad news?"

Everett's expression turned dark.

"There's a book missing," he said in a low voice that showed as much embarrassment as worry. "I discovered it while hunting for Boggin stories. One of the unfinished stories is gone."

"Why is that so bad?" I asked.

"Because it was the last story written about the Boggin. It means you're in the middle of a second tale. That's two stories we're dealing with here. There's more at stake than I imagined, and without that book there's no way of knowing the extent of it."

"How can a book be gone?" Lu asked. "Don't you keep track?"

"If you're asking if I pass out library cards and stamp a return date inside each book, no," Everett said patiently.

"Then we'll never find it," I said.

Everett took off his glasses and wiped his eyes. He looked tired. Did spirits get tired?

"Don't be so sure," he said. "I have a pretty good idea of who took it."

"Who?" I asked.

"Your father, Marcus. Your birth father. Jim Roxbury."

It was my turn to get worked up.

"What! When?"

"Had to have been some time before he died," Everett said. "How many years ago was that?"

"Twelve," I said quickly.

"The book's been gone for twelve years?" Lu asked. "That's going to be one hefty late fee."

"Why would he take out a book about the Boggin?" I asked. "Did it get loose back then?"

"It's possible," Everett said. "There's no way to know without that book."

"Why are you so sure it was my father? Maybe one of the other agents took it."

"Impossible," Everett said, shaking his head. "Your father was the last mortal agent of the Library. That is, until the Paradox key was passed on to you."

"What!" I exclaimed. "You mean there aren't a bunch of other agents running around, finishing these stories?"

"There have been many agents over time," Everett replied. "And there will be more. But as of right now, you're it, son."

"Wow," Lu said numbly. "Lucky you."

"So I'm on my own?"

"Not entirely. You've already done something your father did. He brought in friends to help."

He looked to Lu.

I looked to Lu.

Lu looked sick.

"Wow," she said, still numb. "Lucky me."

"I really wish the good news were better than that," I said.

"I'm here to help too," Everett said. "With these books I can give you the history on pretty much every supernatural event that's been written about. The only thing I can't do is leave here."

"Right, because you're a ghost," Lu said with no enthusiasm. "Yikes."

An idea was forming. One I didn't like but couldn't ignore. The more I thought about it, the more it made my stomach twist. I had to sit down on one of the stools because the thought was actually making me dizzy.

"What's the trouble, lad?" Everett asked with concern.

"There may be even more going on here," I said, thinking hard. "My mother and father died twelve years ago. A rogue storm capsized their sailboat. If my father was fighting the Boggin—"

"Oh my God," Lu exclaimed.

I looked to Everett, hoping he had some logical reason to explain why I was wrong.

His sober expression told me otherwise.

"You may be onto something, Marcus," he said softly.

"Is it possible?" Lu asked.

"Yeah, it is," I said flatly. "The Boggin may have killed my parents."

The words echoed through the ancient library.

"We can't know for sure until you find that book," Everett said.

"We will," I said, more to myself than to anybody else. "We have to."

"So where do we start?" Lu asked.

"With the guy who helped my father. Michael Swenor."

"Uh, isn't he, like . . . dead?" Lu asked.

"Yeah. But his wife might know something about the book."

I jumped up and headed for the door.

"Marcus," Everett called. "I know I don't have to say this, but be careful. From what I've read about that creature, well, let's just say it isn't a friendly spirit."

"You're telling me that like it's something I don't already know."

Lu followed me to the door. I was about to open it

when I remembered something. "Wait, we didn't ask about your cousin's story."

"It's okay," Lu said. "One mystery at a time."

"Are you sure?" I asked.

"Yeah, let's deal with one boogeyman at a time."

I nodded a thank-you, then opened the door and stepped back into Lu's bedroom. When she came through, I closed the door behind her, then opened it again right away to show that it now led to her hallway.

"So weird," she said while sticking her head through.

I grabbed my cell phone and punched in Lillian Swenor's number. After four rings an answering machine picked up.

"Hello!" came a cheery man's voice.

I was about to hang up, thinking I'd called the wrong number, but then the truth hit me.

I was listening to the voice of Michael Swenor.

"You've got the Swenors," he said.

A young kid's voice that must have been Alec's came in next. "Please leave a message after the beep. Bye!"

My brain locked. I had just heard the voices of a happy father and son who had no idea that their lives were about to be turned inside out. Or, in Michael's case, ended.

"Say something," Lu ordered.

"Uh, hi, Mrs. Swenor. This is Marcus O'Mara. I'm

trying to hunt down a book that belonged to my father. My birth father. I was hoping maybe he gave it to your husband for safekeeping. It's pretty important, so if you know anything about it, could you please call me at this number?"

I hit the End button and stared at the phone.

"Okay, what do we do now?" Lu asked.

"I should go home. Tomorrow's Saturday. I'll think about it and call you in the morning."

"Think fast," Lu said.

Lu led me downstairs, but I didn't leave right away because there was something else that had to be said.

"I, uh—I'm sorry, Lu. I shouldn't have gotten you involved. I just didn't know who else to turn to."

"I was already involved, because I'm your friend. It's not like you have a whole lot of 'em."

"Gee, thanks," I said sarcastically, but she was right.

"Besides," she added, "maybe the Library can help me too."

"I hope so. Stay close to your family tonight. Safety in numbers."

"You too. It's not a good time to be at war with your parents."

"I'm always at war with my parents," I said. "Today isn't any different."

"Yeah, but now you're fighting something a lot scarier."

She was absolutely right. I was at war, and everyone I knew and cared about was in the middle of it, thanks to me.

I could only hope I was up for the fight.

CHAPTER
14

The sun was long gone, and the street was dark.

As I stepped away from Lu's house, I knew it was going to be a terrifying walk home. I kept looking over my shoulder, expecting to see the hideous face of that monster old lady as she crept up on me from behind. Every time a car drove by, I hid behind a tree and watched until it passed. A chilly late-fall breeze shook the tree branches, making them look like gnarled claws trying to reach down to snatch me up.

Expecting something scary to happen is the worst kind of torture. Every shadow becomes a ghost; every sound is a potential danger. By the time I got to my house, I was a mess. My heart was racing, and I was out of breath, even though absolutely nothing strange had happened.

And then my cell phone rang. It was Theo.

"Hey," I said. "I'm just getting home and—"

"She's here," Theo said in a strained whisper that sounded like nothing I'd ever heard come from him.

I stopped short at my front door.

"What do you mean? Who's there?"

"It's her," he said, sounding as though he was on the verge of tears. "She's downstairs talking to my parents right now."

My mind went into hyperdrive, trying to understand what this could mean.

"Did you talk to her?"

"No. As soon as I saw her, I ran upstairs and hid in my room," he whispered, on the edge of panic. "I'm under my bed. I don't know what to do, Marcus. If you don't give her the key, more will die. That was her threat, right?"

"Nobody's gonna die," I said adamantly. "I'm coming over. Keep talking."

The McLeans lived only a few blocks from me. I covered the distance in record time as I sprinted along the sidewalk with my cell phone pressed to my ear, listening to Theo's nervous breathing.

"Go to the door, Theo," I said. "Listen to what she's saying."

"I can't," he cried, whining like a terrified two-year-old. "Please, I don't want anything to happen to my family. Or to me."

"It's not you she's after," I said, breathless. "It's me."

"It's not you, it's the key! Just give her the stupid key!"

My gut churned as I heard the fear in Theo's voice. This was my fault. I didn't want anybody to get hurt, but giving up the key would be like making a deal with the devil. What horror might be unleashed if that demon took control of the Library?

"Something's happening," Theo said, his panic amping up. "I think the house is shaking. What is going on?"

"Hang on, I'm almost there," I said as I crossed another street and hopped over the curb to the sidewalk.

"It feels like—oh my God, Marcus, it's an earthquake!"

"Get out of there!" I commanded. "Now! Run down those stairs, grab your family, and get out of the house."

"She won't let us," Theo cried.

"She's a spirit, Theo. She can't stop you. Get out of the house!"

"I'm too scared!"

I rounded the final corner and saw Theo's house. It looked pretty much like ours, with two stories and a

154

lawn in front. I didn't feel the ground shaking, but I did see that the lawn was strangely high, as if it hadn't been mowed in months. Thick green grass covered even the walkway that led up to the front door. That wasn't like the McLeans.

"It might not be real, Theo, but you can't take the chance," I said into the phone. "Get out from under that bed and—"

A violent wind suddenly kicked up, flattening the grass and nearly knocking me over.

Crack!

The thick branches of a massive oak tree next to the house were bent back, straining against the wind. The centuries-old tree fought against the powerful force as hundreds of leaves were instantly torn off and blown away, stripping the branches bare.

"You gotta get outta there, Theo!" I screamed into the phone as I ran for the house.

I plowed through the tall grass, got halfway to the door, and tripped over something that was hidden deep down in the thick growth. I went sprawling forward and landed on my chest. Hard. The force of the fall knocked the wind out of me. As I lay there, gasping for air, I felt something pull at my feet. Whatever it was that I'd tripped over, it wasn't done with me. It felt as though hungry hands were grabbing at my ankles to try and pull me away from the house. I kicked back at the unseen force, desperate to get away.

Crack!

The trunk of the giant oak was bent at an impossible angle. There was no way it could stand up to such a powerful force for much longer.

"Theo!" I screamed.

Crack!

The tree lost the battle. With a sharp tearing sound that was loud enough to cut through the howling wind, the tree toppled. The hundred-foot-high oak splintered near its base with a final, gut-rumbling *snap* and fell toward the house.

I stopped fighting to get closer because the tree was looming overhead, falling my way. I rolled away as fast as I could, praying that the tree wouldn't be blown on top of me.

With a monstrous, explosive crash, the tree hit the house and tore through the roof directly over Theo's bedroom.

"Theo!" I shouted into the phone.

No answer.

I struggled back to my feet, kicking away at the unseen hands that grabbed at me from beneath the grass, and ran for the door.

The giant tree rested against the structure at a

forty-five-degree angle. It had destroyed the roof but was stopped from falling flat by the second floor. I didn't want to believe that Theo was hurt. I had to get him out of there.

I finally fought my way to the house and threw open the front door.

"It's Marcus!" I screamed, hoping to see Theo, or his parents, or his brothers and sister rushing out.

Nobody answered.

Or more will die.

That was what the Boggin had threatened.

This really was a war.

I ran straight for the stairs and flew up, two at a time. Theo's bedroom was at the end of a long hallway. When I got to the second floor, I saw no damage. The tree had fallen directly onto Theo's bedroom, and his door was closed.

"Theo!" I called out, fearing he was trapped. Or worse.

I took one step toward his room but stopped when his bedroom door flew open and somebody ran out.

It was Theo. Alive. Unhurt but not yet safe.

"What's happening?" he screamed in panic.

"We gotta get outta here!" I shouted back. "C'mon!"

Theo ran toward me.

"What about my family?" he called.

"We'll find them," I said. "Let's just get downstairs and out of—"

Boom! Boom! Boom!

The doors on either side of the hallway blew off their hinges as if powerful explosions had erupted in each room. Theo was hit by one of the careening doors and knocked against the far wall.

I was so stunned, I couldn't move. What was happening? Before I could get my wits back, heavy vine-like tendrils reached out from each room, snaking into the hallway like monster pythons. They were thick, bark-and-leaf-covered vines that had a mind of their own as they slithered into the hall, seeking their prey.

Theo.

"Marcus!" Theo called in terror.

Theo had been knocked onto his stomach. He tried to get to his feet, but a vine wrapped around his ankle and pulled him back toward his room, dragging him across the floor. It was as if the fallen tree was reaching into the house, groping for victims.

"Help!" he screamed.

That kicked me into gear. I ran down the hallway, jumping over the broken doors and stumbling past the ever-growing vines that continued to fill the hallway. Theo reached out for me, and I grabbed his hand.

"Please don't let it get me!" he cried.

I pulled him toward me with one hand while reaching forward to yank the vines off his leg with the other. As vicious as they were, I was able to tear them free from Theo's ankle and pull him to his feet. We held on to each other for support as we pushed our way back toward the stairs. It was like fighting our way through a dense jungle as the leafy vines continued to grow, filling the hallway. It felt as though every tendril was another hand grabbing at us, trying to pull us back toward whatever fate it had in store.

With a powerful mix of fear and adrenaline, we fought our way to the stairs and hurried down, with the vines chasing us from behind, reaching out, wanting us back. We went straight for the door, blasted outside, and charged through the tall grass until we got to the sidewalk.

Theo fell to the cement walkway, exhausted.

"My family," he called out, breathless.

"I know," I said while digging for my cell phone. "I'm calling 911."

Theo pulled me down so we were on the same level and looked me square in the eye with fear and desperation.

"Give her the key," he begged with tears in his eyes. "Or more will die."

"I will," I said, trying to keep from crying myself. "I will. But first let me get help."

"Good, good, thank you," he said, sounding relieved.

I pulled out my cell phone and was about to enter 911 . . .

. . . when I stopped. I suddenly realized something. My mind raced back over events, trying to understand. Something was wrong, and not just because Theo's house was being engulfed by deadly predator vines.

"Or more will die," I said, and looked down at Theo. "How did you know about that?"

"She's evil," Theo said.

"Yeah, but how did you know she told me that? And used those words? I didn't tell you."

"Yes, you did," Theo whined.

"No, I didn't. How did you know, Theo?"

Theo looked up at me with pleading eyes, then suddenly changed. His face relaxed. The look of fear and panic disappeared. He stopped breathing hard, wiped away his tears, and laughed. He actually laughed. I thought for a second that his mind had snapped.

"How did you know about that, Theo?" I asked, pressing.

Theo sat up straight, gave me a shrug, and disappeared.

He simply vanished.

I heard a voice coming from the house.

"The next time it might be real."

I shot a look to the destroyed house to see a figure standing in front of the open door, surrounded by a jungle of vines.

The Boggin.

"Surrender the key," she said, and raised her hand out toward me.

A dozen emotions took hold of me. Relief was the first, but it was quickly followed by anger. This demon was torturing me. She was evil. She had to be stopped.

"Bite me!" I shouted at her.

"Then you have made your choice," she said, sounding irritated.

The witch's shadowy image transformed into white smoke that drifted skyward. She was trailed by dozens of thick, writhing vines that rose up and followed her like rats following the Pied Piper. The tendrils snaked out of the house and stretched higher, until they too disappeared into the starry night sky.

I looked back to the house to see . . . absolutely no damage. No broken windows. No tall grass. Most important, the giant oak tree stood straight and tall where it always had. Undamaged. I didn't have to look to my phone history to understand that Theo hadn't actually called me.

The whole thing was an illusion staged for my benefit . . . and horror.

"Hey, Marcus!" came a little girl's voice.

The McLeans' Volvo was pulling into the driveway. Mr. and Mrs. McLean were in front, Theo and his little sister, Claire, in back.

Claire leaned out the window, waving at me. "We got pizza left over! Want some?"

Theo got out of the car and walked to me while pulling on his ear. He knew something was wrong.

"No thanks!" I called to Claire.

"Are you okay?" Theo asked. "What are you doing here?"

I couldn't stand the idea of facing Theo just then. He didn't believe that any of this was happening to begin with. How was I going to persuade him to be careful?

"I'm fine," I said. "But we gotta talk. Tomorrow."

"Uh, yeah. You sure you're okay?"

"I'm not even close to okay," I said, and turned away, headed for home . . . with no idea of how I was going to deal with the evil power of the Boggin that seemed to be growing stronger by the minute.

CHAPTER
15

When I finally dragged myself home, I found Mom and Dad sitting in the living room, waiting for me. Dad immediately got up and went for the kitchen.

"I'll start dinner," he said, which was weird, because Mom usually cooked.

"Let's talk, Marcus," Mom said.

Uh-oh. Those words never led to anything good. The last thing in the world I needed just then was to tangle with my mother, but it wasn't like I had a choice. I sat down on the couch across from her without saying a word. What I wanted to do was spill my guts, but I knew she wouldn't believe me and it would only make things worse.

Mom seemed nervous, which wasn't like her.

Normally, she just jumped right in with whatever was bugging her. Now it seemed as though she was struggling to find the right words.

"Things haven't been good between us lately," she said, as if I didn't already know that. "What I want to say is . . . I'm sorry."

Whoa. Didn't see that coming. I was suddenly very interested in what she had to say.

"For what?" I asked with surprise.

"Because of what I said yesterday. I hope you know I didn't mean that. I was angry, and it was wrong."

All I could do was shrug, because, to be honest, I think she meant it.

"We all have expectations of one another," she said. "But it's unfair to judge anyone based solely on that. I'm not saying I totally approve of all the things you've done, but I want to try to be a little more open-minded. You're growing up, Marcus. Your father and I are doing our best to guide you until the time comes when you don't need us anymore. Until then, I'm going to try to listen more than I have."

I sat there, stunned. Though it sounds impossible, all thoughts of the Boggin were suddenly gone. My mother had never been this open with me. Heck, she'd never admitted she was wrong before. About anything. Ever.

No wonder she was having trouble finding the right words.

"I, uh, I don't know what to say," I finally muttered. "I know you think I do things just to annoy you, but I don't. Not all the time, anyway."

She actually chuckled at that.

"I know. And I can be easily annoyed. It works both ways."

"What does Dad think?" I asked.

She looked off toward the kitchen. I looked too and saw Dad quickly duck his head back around a corner. Busted. He'd been listening.

"He's the one who pointed out how difficult I've been. I guess I don't always listen to him either, but I did this time. I promise you we're going to try, and I hope you will too."

"What changed?" I asked.

"I don't know," she said with a shrug. "I just felt like we were losing you."

Those words hit home. As much as we had been at each other's throats, I always saw us as a family. The idea that it might not last never entered my mind. Not seriously, anyway. I suddenly saw the possibility of flying on a trapeze without a safety net, and I didn't like it.

I think Mom was actually holding back tears.

"I don't want you to change, Marcus. I just want us to be honest with one another."

"Then I've got some bad news for you," I said.

She straightened up.

"What?" she asked anxiously.

"Mr. Winser deserved what he got. If I had the chance to do it over again, I'd do the exact same thing. That's being totally honest."

She laughed. She actually laughed.

"I guess you're pretty good at battling bullies," she said. "Maybe that's a good thing." She stood and added, "Bullies may be fair game, but take it easy on sweet little old ladies, okay? Let's see what your father is cooking up."

As she walked off, reality came rushing back.

That sweet little old lady wasn't a sweet little old lady.

My thoughts suddenly spun out of control. My mother had done something next to impossible by admitting she was wrong and asking us to be honest with each other. But telling her the truth about Miss Bogg and the Library was the last thing I wanted to do. I feared that drawing my parents into this would only put them in more danger. The memory of Theo's house being destroyed by a predator tree was all too real, even though it really wasn't.

After dinner I went to bed early. I wasn't tired, but

I needed to think. What was I going to do? How was I going to defend everyone against that vicious old boogey-lady? I lay there desperately trying to come up with an idea, but all I did was fall asleep.

I didn't wake up until sunlight was streaming through my window. After sleeping all night, I wasn't any closer to a plan of action than when I had left Lu's house the night before.

I jumped out of bed, threw on some clothes, and went right downstairs.

"Mom? Dad?"

No answer. It was Saturday. They usually went out early and did chores. That was good. As long as they were around other people, there was less chance of the Boggin paying them a visit. Or so I hoped. I was about to head into the kitchen to grab some breakfast when . . .

. . . the doorbell rang.

I jumped. Nobody just dropped in on a Saturday morning. At least nobody I knew. Both Theo and Lu slept until noon on Saturdays.

I reached for the key around my neck. I could be out of there in a heartbeat by running up to any door and jumping into the Library.

The bell rang again.

My heart pounded.

I had to know who it was.

Slowly, I walked toward the front door. Next to it was a window. I took a peek out, but the angle was too sharp, and I couldn't see who was standing there.

Knock, knock.

I jumped again.

Whoever was there wasn't going away.

I had to face them.

I stepped right up to the door and listened. For what, I didn't know.

"Who is it?" I called out.

"Marcus?" It was a lady's voice.

It wasn't an old lady's voice either.

"Who's there?" I asked.

"It's Lillian Swenor."

I couldn't open the door fast enough.

Mrs. Swenor stood there, looking every bit as worked as she had in her apartment. Dangling from her hand was a very big shopping bag.

"You got my message," I said.

"I did."

"Please tell me there's a book in that bag."

Mrs. Swenor and I stood there, looking at one another, for an awkward couple of seconds.

"Is it all right if I come in?" she asked sheepishly.

"Yeah, yeah, of course," I said, and stepped away from the door to let her into the house.

I kept staring at the bag, hoping to catch a glimpse of an old-fashioned book.

"Are your parents home?" she asked.

"No," I said while staring straight at the bag.

"I don't have the book, Marcus," she said.

My heart sank. Dead end.

"But I've seen it," she said.

"Really?" I exclaimed with soaring hope. "Where is it?"

"I don't know."

Crash. Another dead end.

"When you came to the apartment, I didn't tell you everything," she said. "I thought I was protecting you. And Michael. But after you called about the book, I decided it would be wrong to hide anything from you."

My emotions kept bouncing from hope to disappointment, then back to hope again. I led her into the living room, where we sat across from one another. The whole time I kept stealing glances at the bag, wondering what she'd brought.

She sighed and said, "I told you that after your parents died, Michael didn't talk about ghosts or strange happenings again. Not for twelve years, anyway. I'd forgotten all about it until last week. Michael got a call from someone who knew your father from the old days. Whatever that person said, it truly upset him."

"Who was it?" I asked anxiously.

"I don't know. Michael wouldn't tell me. But he went to see this person, and when he came home, he wasn't just upset anymore. He was scared."

Tears welled up in her eyes as she related the painful memory.

"He kept saying how he'd done something terrible, something he thought was right, but it turned out to be horribly wrong. Michael was a guy who ran into burning buildings, Marcus. Nothing scared him. But on that day he was terrified. He had an old book with him and kept flipping through the pages. Whatever he was looking for, he couldn't find it and kept slamming the book shut in frustration. I think maybe it was the book you're looking for."

"But you don't know where it is?"

She shook her head.

"Did he tell you what he did that was so bad?"

"Sort of. It made no sense to me, but it tore him apart."

"What was it?"

"He said he broke the seal."

I jumped up as if I'd been hit by a jolt of electricity.

"That's what he said? He broke the seal?"

"Yes. Does that mean something to you?"

It meant everything. I looked to the shopping bag.

"Mrs. Swenor," I said cautiously, "what's in there?"

"Michael brought this home with him that day. I think this is what he broke the seal on."

My stomach turned upside down.

"Can I see it?" I asked.

She reached into the bag and lifted out a plain-looking olive-green metal box about as big as an oversized shoe box. I recognized it from old movies as an ammunition box from World War II. It was battered and scratched, with white, painted-on letters that were mostly chipped off.

"Michael called it a vessel," she said. "He told me your father sealed it just before he died."

"My father?" I said, stunned. "He said my father sealed it? Are you sure?"

"Yes. Do you know what that means?"

I knew exactly what it meant and what the box was. There had been lots of them throughout time. The first was a copper box that was made a few thousand years ago. But the vessel didn't need to be made of copper. All it needed was a copper seal.

Everett was right. My father was dealing with the Boggin when he died. He sealed the demon inside this box twelve years ago. This was its last prison. And a week ago Michael Swenor broke the seal to release it back into the world.

"It's, um, it's . . ." I couldn't think of the right thing to say. I couldn't just say, *That was where my father had the boogeyman trapped, until your husband let it loose.*

"I'm not really sure," I said, lying.

"What was sealed in there?" she asked, with more than a little desperation. "Some kind of disease?"

That was a pretty good guess, but I didn't share that with Mrs. Swenor.

"Finding that book might help solve the mystery," I said.

"I'm sorry, Marcus," she said. "I didn't tell you any of that because I didn't want Michael being remembered for having lost his mind. But you knew about the book. You know it's real. I can only hope that whatever Michael did, it was for a good reason and he didn't realize how badly it would turn out."

"I think that's exactly what happened," I said. "Getting that book would help prove it."

Mrs. Swenor wiped her eyes and stood up.

"If I learn anything more, I'll let you know," she said. "And I'll keep looking for the book."

"Is it okay if I keep the box?"

She glanced down at the old green metal box, and her focus sharpened.

"I don't ever want to see it again," she said with disdain.

With that, I walked her to the door. She left, and I was alone.

As soon as the door closed, I spun around and ran for the box. I picked it up and gave it a thorough once-over to find . . . nothing. There was absolutely nothing unusual about it. It was just an old metal box . . . where my father had trapped the Boggin twelve years ago. Was that the story in the missing book? Was it the story of my father's war with the Boggin?

Was that why he and my mother died?

The vessel had gone missing for twelve years and suddenly turned up about a week ago. Where had it been? Who was the guy who contacted Michael Swenor about it? Why did Swenor break the seal and release the demon? Doors were suddenly opening, but they were only leading to more questions. Most important, the Boggin was still out there, threatening to hurt the people I cared about.

It was going to be a long day.

With the box under my arm, I went into the kitchen to hunt for some breakfast. On the counter was a note.

Morning! Mom and I went to the marina to do a little work on the boat. Maybe we'll go out for a short sail; it's a beautiful day. Dad.

The marina. The boat. We had a twenty-seven-foot Catalina sailboat. My parents spent most every weekend during the nice-weather months sailing on Long Island Sound.

My heart rate spiked. There was nothing good about

this news. It was on a sailboat that my biological parents died. I dropped the box, pulled out my cell phone, and called my mother. My father never took his cell on weekends, but Mom was wired to hers 24-7.

The phone rang. And rang. And rang again. Finally, I got voice mail.

"Mom," I said, trying not to sound too frantic. "I, uh, I want to go with you. Don't go out without me. I'll wait for your call."

I disconnected and immediately sent her a text: *Call me!*

She probably had her cell phone in her bag and couldn't hear it. I wasn't even sure what I was going to tell them. I just wanted to keep them from going out on the water. Not with the Boggin on the loose.

The Boggin.

I looked at the vessel that had once contained it. It was just a box. The box needed a seal.

A copper seal.

I grabbed it and ran for the kitchen and the stairs that led to our basement. Dad's workshop was down there. He had to have something made of copper that I could use as a seal to lock the vessel.

That is, if I could get the Boggin into it. How the heck was I supposed to do that?

Our basement was filled with a collection of old

furniture covered in tarps, outgrown bikes, sleds, garden equipment, and tools. It was a mess. I clicked the light on and ran down the rough-hewn wooden steps, headed straight for Dad's workbench. Dozens of tools were hung neatly on a wire rack above the work surface. Underneath the table were dusty cardboard boxes of junk that I quickly pulled out and dug through. There were random electric switches and plumbing fixtures and painting supplies and absolutely nothing made of copper.

On top of the bench was a square organizer with a bunch of small drawers full of screws and nails and washers. I pulled each one out, hoping to find anything made of copper. In one of the drawers, I actually found a ring of old-fashioned keys that were the same size as the Paradox key. They probably were for the ancient dressers that Dad stored in the basement. None were made of copper.

I was feeling helpless. Even if I found something, how would I get a centuries-old spirit to go inside the vessel? I felt the Paradox key around my neck. If anybody could help, it was Everett. Maybe he'd found something in one of his books that would tell me how to coax a demon into the very same prison it had just escaped from.

I pulled the leather cord up over my head and grasped the key. I could use it on the door at the top of the basement stairs to enter the Library. I spun around, ready to run up . . . and stopped short.

Standing at the foot of the stairs was Miss Bogg.

I was so surprised I jumped back and slammed into the workbench, rattling the rack of tools.

"Enough," the old demon said sweetly. "Surrender the key."

C H A P T E R

17

The Boggin stood between me and the stairs . . . the only way out.

I slipped the Paradox key into the pocket of my jeans, whatever good that would do.

"Leave me alone," I said. Pretty feeble, I know, but it was all I could come up with.

The old lady tilted her head and gave me a sweet smile that made her look like somebody's darling old grandma.

"I would be delighted to, child, once you surrender the key."

She took a step forward, which made me back into the tool bench again and knock a hammer off the rack. In desperation I grabbed it off the bench and flung it at her.

The demon didn't even blink. The hammer passed right through her as if she weren't actually there. It hit the stairs behind her and bounced down at her feet.

"What were you expecting?" she asked coyly. "Flesh and bone?"

"But if you're a . . . a . . . spirit, how can you even use the key?"

Instantly, Miss Bogg transformed into vapor. It was so quick and so stunning that I let out a gasp. The white cloud hung there for a moment, but it wasn't a cloud. It was her. The cloud dropped down to the floor as if pushed by an overhead fan. It swirled around the hammer I had just thrown, and grew dense. With no warning the hammer rose off the floor and flew toward my head. I ducked, and it smashed against the wall of tools behind me, sending more crashing to the bench. I glanced back briefly at the damage, and when I spun around again to face the Boggin, she had returned to human form.

"I do have physical abilities," she said with a smug smile. "Now. Please. Simply place the key on the floor and step away."

"Why?" I asked in frustration. "I don't understand why you want to destroy the Library so bad."

"The agents of that library bring solace to the haunted," she said, turning cold. "They eliminate mystery, uncertainty, and fear . . . everything I was conjured to create. I have done battle with them for centuries, and I tire of their meddling."

"Did you kill my father and mother?" I asked.

Miss Bogg gave me a sinister smile.

"Not knowing the truth haunts you, doesn't it?" She chuckled, as if taking pleasure from my pain.

This monster really did exist to create misery.

"I could erase your doubts and end your constant wondering," she said. "But first you must surrender the key."

She motioned for me to put it down on the floor so she could swoop over in a fog to take it away.

It was tempting, but . . .

"No," I said with finality.

I felt something tickle the back of my neck. I swatted it.

"You have no purpose," I said. "The druids conjured you to create fear in children. It was a mistake. Even they knew it."

"Yet here I am," she said. "With an unquenchable thirst. I exist to create fear. I feed on it. It strengthens me. My powers have grown over the centuries, and now I am capable of so much more."

I felt another tickle on my neck and swiped at it again. It felt as though an annoying mosquito was buzzing me.

"But you're not powerful enough to take the key

from me," I said. "That means it must have some pretty serious power of its own."

She didn't move.

I felt another tickle, this time on the top of my head. I swiped at it and looked at my hand to see three spiders, each the size of a nickel. They were black and furry and very active. They scrambled across my palm and tried to shoot up my sleeve. I had to shake my arm to get rid of them.

"You are an annoying child," she said with disdain. "I enjoy annoying children."

Instantly, I felt something fall on my head. And my arms. And all around me. I swiped them away, but more fell on me. Many more. Looking at my arms, I saw hundreds of spiders scampering across my shirt. They crawled down my collar and tickled my back. I couldn't help but look up. They dropped from the dark rafters of our basement like an army of commandos on zip lines. It was impossible, but they were there. And they kept coming. By the thousands. They swarmed around my face, trying to get into my mouth and eyes. No matter how fast I swept them away, more followed.

Miss Bogg watched calmly.

"You can end this," she said. "Surrender the key."

My body was crawling with spiders. Literally. They weren't satisfied with just landing on me; it was as if they were on a mission to burrow into my skin as they scrambled into every opening in my clothing. My sleeves, the cuffs of my pants, my collar—all were entry points for this army of vicious creatures.

The only things keeping me from going out of my mind were the memories of the impossible images I had seen: a ladder that wasn't there, a bull that disappeared, a storm that wasn't real, and a house that had been crushed by a predator tree . . . until it wasn't.

The Boggin dealt in fear created by illusion.

"They're not real!" I screamed while brushing off the spiders that actually seemed pretty real at the moment. They crawled over my skin, burrowed through my hair, and dug into my scalp.

"None of this is happening!" I screamed.

I fell to the floor and rolled, hoping the motion would crush some of the little monsters before they could sting me. Or bite. Or whatever it was that spider illusions did.

I hated spiders. Did she somehow get into my head to figure that out?

Miss Bogg loomed over me.

"Michael Swenor is dead," she said. "As are your parents. Is that not real?"

"You tricked them," I cried. "I can fight it. I can fight you."

The spiders kept coming. They hit the floor and

instantly skittered my way. These were not mindless creatures. They had a target. Me. There were so many of them swarming all over me that it looked as if I was wearing a fur bodysuit. The tickling against my skin made me want to scream, but I held it back. I didn't want to give that demon the satisfaction.

The Boggin leaned down toward me and said through clenched teeth, "Perhaps *you* can fight me, but can you say the same for your new parents?"

The evil gleam in her eye put me over the edge. I finally let out a scream. It was a desperate cry, filled with terror and anger. She was going after my parents, just as she had my birth parents twelve years before.

History was about to repeat itself.

I lunged at her, hoping to grab her wrinkled old neck. This wasn't an old lady. It was a monster wearing a twisted disguise. She was an evil Mother Goose who told tales of terror. I reached up with my spider-covered hands and grasped at her neck. I had her. I closed my hands, expecting to feel flesh and bone. All I got was air. In that instant she disappeared in a white wisp of fog. It surprised me, but only for a second. This was a phantom. A specter. She wasn't flesh and blood, and she was gone.

The spiders weren't.

I screamed again in absolute, mind-bending anguish,

jumped to my feet, and ran for the stairs. All I could think to do was get out of that dark basement and into the light of my yard. My normal yard. The spiders had other plans. They nipped at my skin like a thousand tiny pinpricks, all striking at the same time, making me feel as though I were being electrocuted.

I screamed again. I couldn't help it. I tripped up the stairs, falling once to my knees, but I got right back up and kept going. I threw open the basement door and sprinted through my house to the front door. I didn't know what being outside would do, but it was better than being trapped inside with a thousand tiny marauders. I got to the door, grabbed the knob, yanked it open . . .

. . . and came face to face with Lu and Theo.

They were as surprised as I was.

"Whoa, are you all right?" Theo asked.

Dumb question. I pushed past them and jumped off my front step, continuing to swipe off the spiders.

"Marcus, what are you doing?" Lu yelled.

I continued to brush at my arms until I realized it was no use. The spiders were gone. It still felt as though they were crawling on my skin, but I was fighting with a memory.

"I . . . I . . . there were spiders," I said, frantic. "Thousands of them."

Theo and Lu gave each other worried looks.

"I know you're afraid of them," Theo said. "But don't you think this reaction is a little extreme?"

I fought the urge to continue brushing them off and focused enough to realize I wasn't even feeling them anymore.

"It was an illusion," I finally managed to say while gasping for breath. "She was here."

"The Boggin?" Lu asked.

I nodded. My mind was already racing ahead to try to understand what had happened and what it meant.

"My parents," I said, and pulled out my cell phone.

I entered Mom's number and once again got her voice mail.

"The Boggin's going after them!" I shouted in a panic. "Lightning's about to strike twice."

I sprinted back into the house.

Lu and Theo were right on my tail.

"Maybe my cell phone isn't getting through to them," I said frantically. "I'll try the home phone."

I ran straight for the kitchen, grabbed the phone, and punched in Mom's number.

"Where are they?" Theo asked.

"At the Tod's Point marina. They're going sailing."

"Ooh, not good," Lu said.

The phone rang. . . . I got Mom's voice mail again and slammed the phone down in frustration.

"Take a breath, man," Theo said.

I forced myself to calm down and focus.

"Do you know what's going on?" I asked Theo.

"Lu explained it all. That's why I'm here, Marcus. Somebody's got to be the voice of reason. There's nothing supernatural going on here."

Theo was dead serious. I looked to Lu.

Lu shrugged and said, "He doesn't buy it."

"There are no such things as ghosts and magic," Theo said slowly and clearly, as if to a child. "If you keep thinking that way, you'll never get to the real reason behind what's happening."

It took every ounce of willpower I had to keep from lunging at Theo, grabbing his shirt, and throwing him against the wall.

"You know it's not just me, right?" I said through gritted teeth. "Lu's been to the Library too. We can't both be having the same hallucination."

"I believe she thinks she's been somewhere," Theo said. "You both do. But a supernatural library run by ghosts? Seriously?"

I grabbed the Paradox key from my pocket and held it up to Theo's face.

"Let's go. Right now. I'll take you there. Come on!"

I stormed over to the back door, ready to use the magic on it.

"No!" Theo shouted.

His voice stopped me cold. I'd never heard him yell like that. He stood there awkwardly, unable to look me in the eye. Something was definitely off.

"What's going on, Theo?" Lu asked softly. "I know you're being all logical about this, but at some point you've got to open your mind to the possibility that something strange is happening."

Theo started shaking. Truly shaking. This was a guy who was always calm and in control. It was as though he was battling with himself to keep from exploding.

"I won't accept it," he finally said, though the words didn't come easily. "I can't. I know how the world works. This doesn't fit."

"That's the whole point," I said. "The Library exists because sometimes things don't fit."

"No," Theo said adamantly, as if trying to convince himself. "If I believed that, I'd have to believe—"

He didn't finish the sentence.

"You're not telling us something, Theo," Lu said. "Why have you been fighting this?"

Theo wiped his forehead nervously and tugged on his ear.

"If I let myself believe in this library, I'd have to accept that I'm going through my own—what did you call it? Disruption?"

Whoa.

Lu and I exchanged surprised looks.

"What does that mean?" I asked. "Did something happen to you?"

Theo sat down at the kitchen counter. He couldn't look at either of us.

"I don't know," he said hesitantly. "Maybe."

"Just tell us," Lu said.

Theo spoke slowly and carefully, as if he wanted to make sure everything he said was fully understood.

"About a month ago, I went to Playland Amusement Park with my older brothers. We found an arcade, where they had one of those silly fortune-telling machines with the dummy of an oracle inside who picks a card out of a box to tell your fortune. It was ridiculous but we all did it. My oldest brother went first. The fortune on his card read *Beware of the bite.* My other brother's said *You will receive good fortune from an unexpected source.* We laughed and forgot all about them until the next day."

He took a troubled breath.

"What happened?" Lu asked.

"The next day my oldest brother was running through the park. He saw a friend walking his dog. When my brother reached out to pet it, the dog bit his hand. He needed ten stitches. That dog never bit anyone before."

"That's just a coincidence," Lu said.

189

"Later that same day, my other brother found out he'd been awarded a four-thousand-dollar scholarship to go toward college tuition. He hadn't even applied for it."

"Okay, a little weirder," Lu said.

"What was your fortune, Theo?" I asked.

Theo slowly reached into his back pocket and took out his wallet. He was moving so slowly, it seemed as though the effort was painful. From out of the wallet he pulled a card and handed it to Lu. Lu read it . . . and gasped.

"Oh my God," she said, breathless.

She looked to Theo; he kept his eyes on the floor. Lu handed the card to me. I read it. Then read it again. I understood the words but wished I didn't.

It said: *Life as you know it will end on your fourteenth birthday.*

"Oh man" was all I could say.

"That's why I can't accept that these disruptions are real," Theo said. "It isn't how life works. There is no magic. Machines can't predict the future. Nothing is going to happen to me on my birthday."

I thought Lu was going to burst out crying, and that's saying something. Lu wasn't the crying type. I didn't feel so hot myself.

It turned out that all three of us were in the middle of our own disruptions.

"Look, Theo," I said. "I don't know if this fortune-telling thing is real or not. It could just be a couple of strange coincidences. But after all the things I've seen, I know for sure that crazy stuff happens, and you can't make it go away by denying it. People have died. That's real, and I'm not going to let anything else bad happen just because it doesn't make logical sense. And you shouldn't either."

Theo pulled on his earlobe. His analytical mind was in overdrive as he tried to come up with rational reasons as to why we weren't actually dealing with the supernatural.

He couldn't.

"I'm scared," he finally said.

"We all are," Lu said. "What are we going to do about it?"

Theo finally looked up at us.

"You really believe this is about an evil spirit that feeds on fear?" he asked.

"I do," I said with authority. "And I believe if there's a disruption that caused Lu's cousin to disappear, and that'll cause you to get a nasty fortune, then we'll find those stories in the Library. And finish them. The way they should be finished."

"How can you be so certain?" Theo asked.

"Because we know how things *should* work. We

191

know what's supposed to happen. I don't care what mystical forces are at work. This is still the real world, and we can use real-world logic to fight back. And you know what? There's nobody who'd be better at that . . . than you."

Theo sat up a little straighter.

Lu actually smiled.

"Please help me save my parents," I said.

Theo looked between the two of us, then tugged on his ear and said, "All righty, Marcus, what can I do?"

I clapped him on the back and said, "Come with me."

I ran across the kitchen, to the stairs that led down to the basement.

"I'm not going back down there alone," I said.

We went down together. There were no spiders or spider bodies anywhere. Illusions don't leave remnants. But the fallen tools were still on the bench, along with the hammer that nearly clocked me. That much was real. I led them to the workbench and picked up the metal box. The vessel.

"Twelve years ago my biological father crossed paths with the Boggin. Somehow he trapped it in here. It was locked inside for twelve years, until Michael Swenor broke the seal and released it."

"Michael Swenor released it?" Lu exclaimed. "Why?"

192

"I don't know. He thought he was doing the right thing, but it backfired, and he paid the price. The Boggin killed him trying to get the key to the Library. It failed, and I got the key instead. Now the Boggin's been haunting me, and it's going after the people I care about to force me to give up the key."

"So how do we stop it?" Theo asked.

"We trap it back in here," I said. "In its spirit form. Once it's inside we seal it with copper. That's how it's worked for centuries. I came down here looking for something copper but came up empty."

Theo took the box from me. He examined it, squinting, deep in thought, pulling at his earlobe.

"It doesn't have to be a real lock?" he asked. "I mean, with a combination or a key?"

"We're talking spiritual power," Lu said. "The book said copper is the Boggin's weakness. It's about the material, not the physical strength of the lock."

Theo ran his fingers across the box's latch, which had a slot for a padlock.

"As long as it's pure copper, all it needs to do is seal this latch?" he asked.

"I think," I said. "Sounds simple, but I don't know what to use."

"I do," Theo said with confidence.

He handed me the box, reached for the hanging tools, and selected a heavy-duty wire cutter. We followed him upstairs, where he led us into the living room.

"I'm assuming you've got the same setup as most every other house in the civilized world," he said. "You've got to promise me one thing, though."

"What's that?" I asked.

"Don't throw me under the bus with your parents when they find out what I've done. Your mother scares me."

"We're trying to save their lives," I said. "I don't think they'll be upset with anything you do."

Theo went straight for the cabinet that held our TV set. He pulled it away from the wall to reveal the wires that fed it power and data.

"Coaxial cable," Theo said. "It's the standard conduit that carries a cable signal."

He used the wire cutter to clip off a two-foot section of cable.

"Ooh, no," Lu said. "Your parents aren't going to like that."

"Is that copper?" I asked Theo.

Theo held up the thick black cable.

"This isn't," he said.

He expertly clamped the wire cutter around one end

of the cable and stripped off a section of the soft black material to reveal the thin metal wire that was its core.

"But this is," he declared.

He quickly stripped off the rest of the covering and was left with a clean length of wire.

Copper wire.

"Feed this through the latch of that box, and presto, you've got a lock made of copper. As to how you get the spirit inside in the first place, I can't help you."

"I've got an idea about that," I said. "But first I have to make sure my parents are okay."

"My dad's ski boat is at that marina," Lu said. "Only one condition."

"What's that?"

"I'm going with you. Dad will kill me if I let somebody take his boat out without me."

"No. Too dangerous."

"Then you can't have it," Lu shot back.

"Really? You wouldn't let me take it?"

Lu looked ready for an argument but backed off quickly.

"Of course I would. But I want to go with you. Everett said it. You need help."

"I'm going too," Theo said.

"Besides," Lu added, "what if the Boggin realizes

you're going to warn your parents and decides to come after us instead? I think it's better if we all stay together."

I couldn't argue with the logic. I hated putting my friends in danger, but they were already in danger just for being my friends.

"Did you ride your bikes here?" I asked.

"Yup," they both answered.

"Good. It's a mile to the marina."

CHAPTER
19

The three of us rode our bikes furiously though the neighborhood, headed for the marina at Tod's Point. In summer, the narrow access road that twisted through the neighborhood was always choked with shoregoing traffic. Fortunately, it was a chilly October, so the traffic was light.

I tore through intersections without looking for oncoming traffic. I didn't care. People were going to have to look out for me, because I was on a mission. On my back was a pack that held the vessel. I had a vague idea of how I might be able to coax the Boggin inside, but wished I had run it by Everett first, because I had no plan B.

If my idea didn't work, we were sunk.

Theo and Lu struggled to keep up and were nearly hit more than once by cars I'd cut off. I had the sick feeling that I was leading them toward disaster.

We flashed past the guard booth and into the park that held Stony Brook's beach. It was a great place, with acres of wooded trails, a sandy beach, picnic areas, and a marina for small private boats. My legs were screaming tired, but that didn't stop me from pumping even harder. The road snaked around the shoreline for another mile, until it led us to the series of floating docks that was Tod's Point Marina. I sped into the parking lot, scanning for my parents' car, hoping we'd find them packing up.

I found our car, and the three of us skidded to a stop behind it on the sandy blacktop.

My parents weren't there.

"My mother's purse is on the front seat," I said.

"With her phone in it, I'll bet," Lu said.

I pushed off again, pedaling for the docks. Normally, I'd have locked my bike in the rack, but there was no time for that. I jumped off while it was still moving, dumped it, and ran for the shore.

The floating docks were put into the water every spring and taken out in November before the Sound froze over. There were slips for a few hundred small recreational vessels, both powerboats and sailboats.

Running down the interconnected docks was like speed-ing through a labyrinth, but I'd done it enough times to know exactly where I was going. Our slip was on the dock farthest out from shore, with the other fixed-keel boats.

I ran from dock to dock, wending my way closer to ours. It was a chilly morning, so nobody else was there working on their boat. I kept my eyes on the masts of the boats that were tied up side by side, hoping to see ours. I didn't even worry about what I would tell my parents when I got there. All I wanted to do was keep them from going out on the water, where anything could happen.

I made the last turn and sprinted to the end of the final dock to see that . . .

. . . our slip was empty.

I wanted to scream. Or cry. Or hit somebody. None of that would have changed things. My parents were out on the Sound and sitting ducks for the Boggin.

"How long do you think they've been gone?" Lu asked as she and Theo caught up, breathless.

"They probably got here and did some work," I said. "Then they had to rig the sails. It's all a guess, but they probably shoved off about an hour ago."

Theo looked around at the cove, which was an inlet of Long Island Sound. The wind was kicking up ripples on the water.

"There's a good breeze," he declared. "They could be anywhere."

"No, when they go out for a short Saturday sail, they always do the same thing. They loop around Great Captain's Island."

"Then let's go catch 'em," Lu declared.

"Are you sure?" I asked.

Lu got a devilish gleam in her eyes that I saw only when she was ready to do something crazy . . . which was fairly often.

"You're asking me if I want to take my father's ski boat, with a four-hundred-twenty-five-horsepower monster of an inboard engine, and open it up to catch somebody in the middle of the Sound? Do you *know* who you're talking to? Have we met?"

"It's not as simple as that, and you know it," I said.

"Yeah, but you won't let anything happen to us, right?"

She didn't wait for an answer and took off running.

"You didn't answer her," Theo said.

"What can I say? I'm making this up as I go along."

We followed her along the floats, headed for her father's slip.

"Do you really have a plan to catch this thing?" Theo asked.

"Yes," I answered truthfully.

"Care to share?"

"We're going to beat this thing at its own game," I said. I didn't go into any more detail because I didn't want him shooting down the only plan I had.

We ran off the docks that held mostly sailboats and sprinted to the docks that held the powerboats. Lu's father's boat was in a slip on the dock closest to shore. She immediately started unsnapping the canvas cover that protected it. Seconds later she pulled back the canvas to reveal a gleaming yellow-and-white Glastron beauty with seats for four and a sunken deck for two more in the bow. The cockpit looked like something you'd see in a race car. Or a fighter jet.

"Wow," Theo said as the boat was revealed. "It looks fast just sitting there."

"I know, right," Lu replied as she quickly stowed the cover under the rear bench. "You want to be holding on to something when I throttle up."

"Your dad lets you take this out on your own?" Theo asked.

"It's an ongoing debate," Lu replied. "He won't let me take it out alone until I prove I can do it, but I can't prove it unless I take it out on my own."

"So what does that mean?" I asked.

"It means I'm about to prove it."

"Don't you have to be sixteen to take a high-powered boat out without an adult?" Theo asked.

"You going to turn me in?" Lu asked coyly.

"No, but you can handle this thing, right?" Theo asked in a shaky voice.

Lu reached under the dashboard and took out the ignition key. She slipped it into the ignition and turned it. The monstrous inboard engine responded instantly and roared to life.

She looked at us with a devilish smile.

"Oh yeah," she said. "I can handle this."

Theo gave me a nervous look. "I don't know what worries me more, getting in this monster with her or facing the boogeyman."

"Cast off," Lu commanded.

Theo jumped on as I untied the bowline that was secured around the cleat on the dock and tossed the rope on board. With a quick shove I got the craft moving back out of the slip and hopped aboard.

Lu stood at the wheel, looking confident. She eased the craft out slowly, being sure not to bounce off the nearby boats. When we were clear, she reversed the engine, and we were under way.

"I'm supposed to go slow until we're out of the cove," Lu said. "Coast Guard rules. Can't make a wake."

I wished she wouldn't be so cautious.

I got my wish.

"But under the circumstances . . . ," she said, and pushed the throttle forward.

We didn't launch, but we definitely sped along faster than the Coast Guard would have liked, creating a wake that jostled all the boats that were moored along the channel.

I took the shotgun seat next to Lu while Theo sat on the bench seat behind us. My pack went on the deck, between my feet. I didn't want to risk losing the vessel over the side once Lu really opened it up.

"So you've got a plan, right?" Lu asked.

"I do. But if anything goes wrong, get away as fast as you can. I don't want to put you guys in any danger."

"I think it's too late to worry about that," Theo said, tugging on his ear.

We zipped past dozens of moored boats, headed for the mouth of the channel and the wide-open Long Island Sound.

"Thank you, guys," I said.

"Don't thank us," Lu said. "We don't want that boogey coming after us, either."

"I know, but this is my battle," I said. "I've lost one set of parents. I don't know what I'd do if I lost another."

Nobody commented on that. I think they were both

imagining themselves in my shoes. The idea of losing your parents was beyond horrible, even if you didn't always get along with them.

"Did you make peace with them?" Lu asked.

"Sort of. My mom made peace with me," I said.

"Go figure," Lu said with mock surprise. "I guess now it's your turn."

We moved along in silence except for the low growl of the engine, which sounded almost angry, as if annoyed by the fact that it was being held back from unleashing its full fury.

It would get the chance soon enough.

The Long Island Sound is a huge body of water that lies between the south shore of Connecticut and the north shore of Long Island. If you travel west, you eventually hit the waterways that surround New York City. To the far east is the Atlantic Ocean. The U.S. Navy berths many of its nuclear submarines out that way, in New London. That's how deep the Sound is. It's like an inland sea.

There's another town beach, on an island about a mile from the marina. It's called Great Captain's Island, and during the summer there's regular ferry service out there. You can't miss seeing it, even from a distance, because there's a big old black-and-white-striped lighthouse on the far shore that towers over the small island.

It's the turnaround spot my parents always use when out for a short sail.

We were about to pass the last of the buoys that mark the channel. Once beyond that, there was no speed limit.

"The Sound is empty," Theo remarked. "Once summer is over, nobody goes out anymore."

"Good," Lu said. "Nobody to get in our way."

When we cleared the last spit of land and the tall trees that grew right up to the shoreline, Great Captain's Island was revealed, along with its unmistakable lighthouse. It seemed so far away.

"That's it," I said. "Head straight for the lighthouse."

Lu gripped the wheel with her left hand and grasped the throttle with her right.

I tensed up.

Lu gave us a look and a sly smile.

"Hold on," she said. "This is going to be fun."

I grabbed on to the seat cushion, and not a moment too soon. When Lu jammed the throttle forward, I was thrown back into the seat like a fighter pilot being launched from the deck of an aircraft carrier. The engine sound shifted from a low growl to pounding thunder. The deck hummed with the surge of energy as we took off and flew over the glassy water.

"Whoa!" Theo exclaimed out of surprise. Or excitement. Or fear.

Lu wasn't exaggerating. It felt as though we were flying.

"It's a calm day," Lu yelled over the fast thumping of the engine. "No swells. We should be there in ten minutes."

The conditions were perfect. The sky was blue, and the wind had died down, so the water was about as flat as I'd ever seen it. It was actually a terrible day for sailing but perfect if you wanted to get somewhere in a hurry and had a few hundred horses pushing you there.

"What are we going to tell your parents?" Theo asked.

"Hopefully, there won't be any trouble and I'll just tell them I was worried they'd be stuck out here with no wind, and offer them a tow."

"And what if there's trouble?" Lu asked.

"Then explaining myself will be the least of our problems."

We shot across the glassy surface for five minutes, watching the island and the lighthouse grow larger as we drew closer. I kept scanning the horizon, looking for anything out of the ordinary. There were no other boats out. Between the lousy wind and the late season, most people must have decided it wasn't worth it. It was just my luck that my parents were the ones who didn't care and went out anyway.

"Grab the binoculars under your seat," Lu called out.

I reached down and pulled out a small pair of black, waterproof binoculars. They may have been tiny, but they had incredible magnification. Holding them up to my eyes, I could make out the windows on the lighthouse.

"Do you see them?" Theo called.

I scanned the water around the island.

"No!" I shouted back.

"Maybe they didn't go there," Lu offered.

I hated to think that was possible, because it meant they could be anywhere. But there was another possibility I liked even less. What if the Boggin had already gotten to them? I pushed that thought out of my head and continued my search.

"Scan the shoreline," I called back to Theo. "Maybe they went up the coast instead."

Theo turned around, got on his knees for balance, and squinted against the sun to try to catch any sign of them along the mainland we were rapidly leaving behind.

"I don't see any sails anywhere," Theo announced.

"They might have dropped them," I called out. "If the wind is really bad, they'd use the outboard motor."

"That would make it really hard to see them," Lu said.

I turned the binoculars back to the mainland, searching for a moving mast. I looked off to our right and then to our left. I spotted a few boats, but they looked to be tied up to moorings. There was no sign of my parents.

"Hey, Marcus," Lu called out. "Do your parents sail all the way around that island before heading back?"

"Yeah!" I yelled.

"Take a look," she called out while pointing ahead.

I spun around and looked through the binoculars to see the sails of a small boat that was clearing the light-house as it appeared from the back side of the island.

"That's them!" I shouted with relief. "I can see two people on board. They were behind the island. They're okay!"

I was never more excited to see my parents. The relief I felt was like having a massive weight taken off my chest.

"I'll head on a course that'll cut them off," Lu yelled. "We should get to them in about five minutes."

I could breathe again.

"Hey, are you crying?" Lu asked.

My eyes were tearing, for sure.

"No!" I exclaimed. "It's the wind."

I sat back in my seat, behind the windshield, and

wiped my eyes. Flying along at that speed really did make it windy, but that wasn't why I was tearing up. Until I saw that my parents were safe, I didn't realize just how truly terrified I was that something might have happened to them. I may have been crying, but they were tears of total relief.

I raised the binoculars to get another look and saw my father peering back at us with his own binoculars. He recognized me and waved.

I waved back. My feeling of relief was complete.

Plink!

Something bounced off the deck in front of the windshield.

"What was that?" I called out.

"I don't know," Lu said. "Something hit us."

Plink! Plink!

Two more small objects hit the deck and bounced into the water.

"I saw that!" I exclaimed, standing up. "What were they?"

"Hail," Theo said as he stepped up between us.

"Hail?" I repeated. "Like, ice from the sky? But it's not even—"

I looked up, and my words caught in my throat.

A huge black cloud had drifted over us.

"Where did that come from?" Lu asked.

"Better question," Theo said. He pointed off our starboard side and said, "What is that?"

Far in the distance, rolling in from the east, was a wall of fog so thick that it looked like a white curtain.

And it was headed our way.

The sky opened up.

A torrent of hailstones fell from the ominous dark cloud, bouncing off the boat, and us, like Ping-Pong balls. Hard, sharp Ping-Pong balls. Along with it came cold, piercing rain.

"I can't see anything," Lu called out with her hand up over her eyes to try to ward off the pelting assault from the sky. "I have to stop."

She throttled back, and after one last push forward from the wake, the speedboat drifted to a standstill.

The barrage of hailstones didn't let up, hitting us hard and stinging our skin. I dug under the back bench and pulled out the canvas covering that had protected the boat in the slip. The three of us held it up like a limp umbrella for whatever lame protection it offered against the deluge.

"Where did this come from?" Theo yelled, wide-eyed.

"Guess," Lu replied. "Did you think we were kidding about the Boggin?"

"The storm is growing," I declared.

The sky darkened as the storm cloud expanded from within like a blooming flower. A giant, gray killer flower.

I lifted the binoculars and looked toward my parents.

The pelting rain and hail had hit them too. They did the smart thing and quickly lowered their sails. While Dad stowed them below, Mom dropped the propeller of the outboard. It was a small, eight-horsepower engine that was mostly used to get in and out of the marina. It didn't offer much speed, but it was better than having sails up in a storm. That would be dangerous.

"They're okay," I announced. "They're headed toward us under power, about a half mile away."

"We can tow them in," Lu said. "I'll motor ahead slowly."

Lu eased the throttle forward, and the propeller kicked in, pushing us gently ahead. The hailstones continued, pounding the canvas covering our heads. The incessant clatter of ice against the fiberglass hull was so loud that I could barely hear our engine.

None of us questioned what was going on or what might happen. All we could do was keep moving.

"Here comes the fog," Theo announced.

The white mist enveloped us quickly. Oddly, as soon as we were engulfed, the rain and hail stopped. I threw the canvas cover off and looked around to see a whole lot of nothing. The fog didn't create a complete white-out, but it obliterated any view of my parents' boat.

"Do you have an air horn?" I asked Lu.

Lu flipped up her own seat and took out an air horn. I grabbed it, raised it into the air, squeezed the trigger, and let out two sharp, ear-piercing blasts.

"Oww," Theo wailed, sticking his fingers in his ears. "A little warning, please."

Ten seconds later my signal was answered by two horn blasts from my parents.

"Yes!" I exclaimed. "We can guide them toward us with the horn. I'll let out a blast every thirty seconds."

"We shouldn't go any faster than this," Lu said. "I don't want to miss them. Or hit them."

"This is good," I said. "We'll reach them soon enough and—"

"Whoa, what is that?" Theo exclaimed.

He walked forward to the bow, looking dead ahead.

I joined him but didn't see a thing.

"All I see is fog," I said.

"The water," he said, the tension in his voice growing. "Something's down there."

He pointed to a spot roughly twenty yards ahead of us. The water was perfectly calm, with no swells or even a ripple from the wind. But the spot he was pointing to, dead ahead, was bubbling.

"Stop!" I shouted to Lu.

She immediately shifted into neutral, then quickly slipped the engine into reverse. The water from our wake flowed around us, coaxing us forward, but the engine fought back until we were once again at a standstill.

Another foghorn sounded. My parents were asking for directions.

I lifted our horn and gave them a sharp return signal, but my attention was on the water ahead of us.

The bubbling grew more intense.

"That's not a natural phenomenon," Theo said.

"It's her," I said soberly.

The bubbling water began moving. It started out slow and very small, but it was plenty dramatic. It was a whirlpool. The water swirled clockwise, creating a funnel-like underwater tornado that quickly grew. And grew.

"Reverse!" I shouted to Lu.

Lu throttled up, and we backed away from the phenomenon.

"I feel the pull," Lu said. "It's trying to suck us in."

"Fight it!" I ordered.

Lu gave the engine more power as the whirlpool continued to grow in size and strength. The movement was so strong that the fog in the air above it began to swirl, creating a strange weather event just for us.

Another sharp horn blast cut through the fog.

I lifted my own horn automatically to respond, but Theo grabbed my arm.

"No," he warned. "You're drawing them right to it."

I turned to Lu and shouted, "Get us outta here!"

Lu didn't have to be told twice. She instantly spun the wheel hard and accelerated to get away from the spinning water.

"We're not moving," she announced. "It's holding us here."

"Gun it!" I commanded.

Lu pushed the throttle back. The engine revved and complained, but we didn't move. We were held in the claws of this swirling monster.

"It's okay," I said hopefully. "It's an illusion. There's nothing to be afraid of. It only looks real."

"I'm not so sure about that," Theo said.

"The Boggin has no physical power," I argued. "It can only create images. We're looking at shadows."

"Really?" he said. "Does this look like an illusion to you?"

He held up his arm to show me a slash that ran across his forearm. Blood welled in the deep wound.

"How did that happen?" I asked.

"I got hit by one of the hailstones. If the Boggin created that storm, it wasn't just an illusion. She has some control over the physical world."

I thought back to the hammer that the Boggin had lifted off my basement floor and flung at me. The rules of this war were changing.

We both looked toward the churning whirlpool, which was now ten yards wide. It was holding us in its grip. Anything caught in that eddy would be sucked down into the depths. I had no doubt that it was big enough, and powerful enough, to bring us down, along with the sailboat that was growing closer by the second.

Was this how my parents had died?

I stood staring at the swirling menace, not knowing what to do. This was my fault. I had put my family and friends in danger. I should have chucked that key and never gone back to that library, no matter what my biological father wanted. Going to the Library turned out to be a tragic mistake for him. And my mother. And the Swenors. Now the people who raised me were headed for the same fate. All because of a weird library that supposedly helped people in supernatural trouble.

In that moment, I didn't care about Everett and his library of unfinished stories.

I cared about my parents.

"Stop it!" I screamed, looking up to the gray sky. "You want the key? Come on! Come and get it!"

"What are you doing, Marcus?" Lu said.

"Where are you?" I shouted to nowhere. "Show yourself. Face me!"

"Marcus, look," Theo said, pointing into the swirling vortex.

A cloud of white mist drifted up from below, moving strangely against the downward spiral of water. It spun in the air and formed a small tornado that moved in the reverse direction of the whirlpool. It wasn't a natural event. The thing was moving with purpose.

The swirling cloud rose up out of the vortex, then floated toward us.

"Tell me again how none of this is real," Theo said nervously as he backed toward the stern of the boat.

I stood with my legs apart, facing it. Whatever the Boggin was sending our way, I wasn't going to back down from it.

The spinning vapor rose up until it was over the bow of the speedboat.

"I can't get away from it," Lu announced.

"Good," I said, standing firm.

The small tornado hovered over the bow as a shadow appeared from within. It grew quickly into a human shape. The vapor blew away, leaving the old woman in the dark-green dress standing on the bow of the boat. Or was she floating?

"Whoa," Theo exclaimed, and fell back onto the bench seat.

"Well, that just happened," Lu said, stunned, as she stood close behind me, peering over my shoulder.

"I . . . I didn't really believe . . ." was all Theo managed to say.

Now he did.

"You can end this, child," the Boggin said in a voice that cut through me like the shrill sound of a knife slicing metal. "Your parents do not have to die."

"They won't die!" Lu shouted. "It's all just shadows."

The sky opened up again, sending a shower of heavy, sharp hailstones raining down on us. They hit. They stung.

"Ow!" Lu screamed. She was hit directly on her forehead by a chunk of ice, opening up a nasty gash. The impact knocked her backward, and she fell on the bench seat, next to Theo.

Though I was being pummeled, I didn't move or flinch. I kept my eyes on the Boggin.

The deluge ended abruptly.

"I have grown strong over the millennia," the Boggin said calmly. "Fear is a powerful weapon that can destroy the strongest of wills."

"Including yours," I said defiantly.

The spirit laughed.

"You don't truly believe that?" she said, scoffing.

"I do," I said. "You can be frightened."

"What could I possibly fear?" she said.

I felt like a fisherman who just got the first telltale tug on his line.

"You're afraid of the Library."

"That library is nothing more than an annoyance," she said harshly.

I'd hit a nerve.

The fish had taken the bait.

"Then why do you want to destroy it?"

"Because I'm tired of the constant attempts to contain me."

"So you *are* afraid of it!"

"There is nothing I fear!" she shouted, her anger rising.

"I don't believe you," I said, taunting her.

I knelt down, pulled the metal vessel out of the backpack, and held it up for her to see.

"You know what this is?" I asked.

It looked as though she stiffened with surprise, ever so slightly.

"You believe the sight of that crude prison is enough to frighten me?"

"No."

I walked a few steps forward and put the metal box down on the deck directly below where she hovered. I kicked open the lid and stood back.

"But the idea of being trapped in there frightens you," I said.

She shook her head dismissively. "Child, I have been imprisoned in vessels similar to that one for centuries at a time. There is nothing about it that frightens me."

"Prove it," I said. "Go inside."

She stared down at the box. For that brief moment she seemed to be nothing more than a scared old woman and not the face of everyone's worst fears.

"I do not need to prove anything to you," she finally said.

The horn sounded from my parents' boat. It made me jump in surprise, for it was getting dangerously close to the spinning waters.

I reached around my neck and grasped the leather cord holding the key. I pulled it over my head.

"Whoa, Marcus, are you sure?" Lu cautioned.

I held the key in my fist and said to the Boggin, "I'm doing this to save them, but you have to work for it. Prove to me that you're not afraid."

"How could I possibly do that?" she asked, almost giddy. Her excitement over getting her hands on the Paradox key was growing.

"I'm surrendering this key to you," I said.

I tossed the key into the box. It hit the bottom with a metallic clatter.

"But you have to go get it."

"Oh man," Lu said, defeated.

The Boggin stared down at the container with a mix of fear and longing. She wanted that key. She needed that key. The Library represented her only challenge on the face of the planet. It was so close.

All she had to do was get it.

Theo and Lu got up and stood behind me. All eyes were on the Boggin, waiting for her to make the next move.

"You think this frightens me?" she said while staring down at the box. "No matter what happens, the final victory will always be mine, for I have something you mortals do not."

"What's that?" I asked.

"Time," she said. "I have existed for thousands of years, and I will exist for thousands more. If there is one thing I have developed, it is patience. I will always be here, waiting, for I have all the time in the world."

The old woman spun around and transformed back into vapor. The black shadow melted into white, and the swirling mist descended toward the vessel.

I held my breath.

Lu grasped my arm and squeezed.

The white cloud shrank down and entered the box.

"Do it!" Theo screamed.

I kicked the lid shut and dove to the deck. In my hand was the copper wire. I quickly slid it through the latch and gave it a twist to make sure it wouldn't fall off.

"Make it tight!" Lu ordered.

I gave it another twist, then stood up and backed toward my friends.

We stood together, staring at the box, waiting for something to happen. Would it bounce? Would it explode? Would the lid flip open, and would the Boggin come flying out like an enraged Tasmanian devil?

"Are you sure that little wire's strong enough to hold it?" Theo asked nervously.

"It's not about how strong it is; it's about what it's made of. Are you sure it's copper?"

"Absolutely," he replied with confidence. "The cable companies use pure copper because it's a great conductor and—"

The green box lit up. A warm light enveloped it, making it glow.

We all took a surprised step backward.

"She's burning it open!" Lu exclaimed.

The warm glow grew brighter, lighting up not only the box but the deck around it.

"At least, I thought it was pure copper," Theo said, his voice quivering.

The light grew so bright that I had to shield my eyes.

"It's okay," I said, and pointed to the sky. "She's not going anywhere."

We all looked up to see the dark clouds breaking apart, allowing rays of sunshine to sneak through. There was no more hail. No more rain. The warm glow wasn't being made by the Boggin. It was sunlight hitting the boat.

The swirling vortex of water in front of us spun out. With a gurgle, the hole disappeared, and the surface of the Sound was once again calm.

"I knew it was pure copper," Theo said, cocky.

"Look!" Lu exclaimed.

A sailboat appeared through the mist ahead of us, off the port bow.

"That was cutting it a little too close," she said, exhaling with relief.

The boat seemed like a ghostly apparition as it appeared from out of the mist.

"Wait," Theo said. "Why are their sails up?"

One look at the boat gave me the answer.

"It's not my parents," I said. "Our boat's way smaller than that."

This sailboat was nearly twice the length of ours. It looked to be a vintage craft, with lots of teak trim and a large silver wheel to the stern. Whereas our boat was designed for short cruises, this beauty looked as though it could navigate more challenging ocean waters.

"Where did they come from?" Theo asked.

The beautiful boat approached us smoothly, several yards off to port. I couldn't take my eyes off it as it cut through the water with its sails perfectly trimmed and filled with wind.

But there was no wind.

Something was off.

"Who's the guy?" Lu asked.

Standing in the very tip of the bow was a man I was surprised to see, only this time I understood why he was there. And I wasn't frightened.

It was Michael Swenor.

He was wearing khakis and a sweater, standard sailing clothes. Unlike the other times I'd seen him, when he'd stared at me with sad, haunted eyes, Michael actually looked relaxed. And happy. As the sleek craft approached, he raised his hand, waved to me, and smiled.

"You know him?" Theo asked.

"I do," I said.

"What's he so happy about?" Lu asked skeptically. "He must have gotten hit by the storm too."

"I think it's because his story is finally complete," I said.

"Oh," Lu said. "Wait, what?"

I waved to Michael with pride, knowing he could now rest in peace.

As the boat swept past, I saw that there were two other people aboard. A man and a woman. The man was at the wheel, toward the stern, and the woman was at his side. His arm was around her waist. Like Michael, both wore boating clothes, looking like a couple who couldn't be happier while out for a morning sail.

And they looked familiar.

As they drew closer and I got a better look at them, I felt certain I'd met them before. They were definitely familiar to me, yet they weren't at all. It wasn't until they were directly across from us, as close as they were going to get, that it hit me.

The guy looked like me. An adult me. He gave me a big smile and a thumbs-up.

The woman blew me a kiss and waved. We were close enough that I could see she was smiling through bittersweet tears.

"You know them too?" Lu asked, incredulous.

I waved back numbly. I wanted to laugh, and shout, and maybe cry a little myself. I felt completely whole and, at the same time, very alone. If there was one overriding emotion that swept over me in that moment, it was pride. I had made them proud.

"They're my parents," I said.

"No, they're not," Theo said, scoffing. "They don't look anything like . . ."

Theo's words caught in his throat as we watched the boat glide past.

". . . ghosts."

The image I will always keep with me is of two happy people out for an afternoon sail with their friend, looking at me with huge, loving smiles.

My father raised two fingers to put bunny ears behind my mother's head.

Then they were gone, disappearing into the mist of the chilly fall day.

"And that just happened," Lu said, stunned.

The harsh sound of an air horn brought us all back to the moment.

Mom and Dad's sailboat puttered up to us as the fog dissipated and bright sunlight painted the surface of the water.

Mom leaned over the side with a line at the ready.

"Are you kids all right?" she called, sounding frazzled.

Theo, Lu, and I exchanged looks and laughed.

"We're fine," I called back. "What about you?"

"Scared to death!" Mom exclaimed as she tossed me the line.

We all worked to bring the sailboat up alongside the powerboat. Dad cut the outboard motor, and we drifted together.

Mom immediately leapt into our boat, threw her arms around me, and hugged me close.

"That was horrible!" she exclaimed. "I was so worried for you kids."

She opened her arms out wider so that Lu and Theo could get the benefit of her motherly hug. They both went along with it while we all exchanged smiles. Nobody rolled their eyes.

"What did you see?" Lu asked. "Hail!" she said. "I'd never been through such a thing. Theo, you're hurt. And, Lu, you've got a cut on your forehead."

"We're okay," Lu assured her. "Just some nicks."

"I'll get the first-aid kit," Mom said.

"That's all you saw?" I asked.

"What else was there to see?" Dad said as he leaned in from the sailboat. "It was pea soup fog. I was

227

afraid we'd ram you. What are you all doing out here, anyway?"

Lu and Theo looked to me. This was my call. I had to answer.

"It was so calm, we thought you'd be stuck out here. That little outboard is useless, so we came out to see if you'd need a tow. We had no idea that storm was going to come out of nowhere."

I exchanged looks with Theo and Lu. They nodded. They got it. I wasn't about to tell my parents the whole story. Especially not since it was over and everyone was safe.

"Well, thank you," Mom said as she pulled away. "You kids are the best."

"Yes, we are," Lu said with a smug smile.

"I'm just relieved we're all safe," Mom said. "But I'm freezing. We've got enough dry sweatshirts for everybody."

She gave us one last squeeze and let us all go. She then took a step toward the bow and accidentally tripped over the metal vessel that was on the deck between the seats.

The three of us gasped, fearing the thin copper wire might break.

I lunged forward and caught Mom before she went crashing to the deck.

"Ow!" she yelled. "I'm such a clod."

"Sorry," Lu said, and quickly picked the box up. "It's a gearbox. Shouldn't have left it out like that."

She shoved it into Theo's arms.

"Don't drop it," she said while staring him down.

"Don't worry," Theo replied.

While Lu and Dad worked to lash together a tow, Mom grabbed both of my shoulders and leaned in close.

"Thank you for coming out here," she said.

"No problem," I said with a casual shrug. "You're my mom. Maybe you still need me too."

I thought I actually saw tears grow in her eyes. She pulled me in and gave me another hug. It was embarrassing, yeah. But that was okay. I guess she was a hugger after all. Theo and Lu weren't about to give me a hard time.

They knew what I had sacrificed to save my parents.

Mom climbed back aboard our sailboat to get the dry sweatshirts and the first-aid kit. It gave Theo, Lu, and me a moment alone.

"I love happy endings," Lu said.

"Me too," I replied. "Except this story isn't over just yet."

CHAPTER
21

Two hours later, Lu, Theo, and I sat together on the end of my bed, staring at the vessel on my desk.

"It looks so innocent," Theo said. "Hard to believe what's trapped inside."

"That wire looks pretty fragile," Lu pointed out.

"We'll fix that," I said. "I don't want anybody to be able to open that ever again."

"You did the right thing, Marcus," Lu said wistfully. "The smart thing. You totally played that monster. But it was a huge price to pay. The Paradox key is locked in there with the Boggin. We'll never enter the Library again. Nobody will. None of the other stories will be finished."

The two looked pretty down. I could read their minds. Lu was thinking about her cousin, and Theo was worried about his fourteenth birthday.

"I hope it was worth it," Theo said glumly.

I stood up and said, "There's actually one more mystery you guys can solve."

"Really?" Lu asked, brightening up.

"What is it?" Theo asked.

"Just how dumb do you think I am?"

The two exchanged confused looks.

"What kind of question is that?" Theo asked.

"Do you really think I was stupid enough to put the *real* key in that box?"

The two sat bolt upright.

I reached into the pocket of my jeans and took out the Paradox key.

They both jumped to their feet with surprise.

"You switched keys?" Lu exclaimed.

"I found a bunch of old keys in the basement when I was looking for copper. That's when I got the idea to trick the old hag."

Theo said, "So the Boggin's stuck in there with—"

"With a key that probably fits some dusty old cabinet in our basement. I don't want to pile on, but I hope she knows it."

"Oh, please, pile on," Lu said. "That is just sweet."

"So this means we still have a shot at finding our own stories?" Theo asked.

I looked at the tarnished brass key and its clover-leaf design. It seemed so normal. It was hard to believe it possessed such amazing power, and magic.

"Absolutely," I said. I went to my desk, picked up the vessel, and turned to my friends.

"Ready?" I asked.

"Now?" Theo exclaimed nervously. "Right now?"

I walked to my bedroom door and felt the familiar warmth pulse from the key. I held it out toward the door, making the keyhole appear.

Theo gasped. "After all I've seen, why am I still surprised?"

"Get used to it," Lu said. "We're still just getting started."

I twisted the key and opened the door to reveal the stacks of books beyond. Theo looked every bit as stunned as Lu had when I first brought her there.

A laugh came from deeper inside. Something had struck Everett as funny.

We hurried past the aisles of books to the circulation desk, where the spirit librarian sat, reading a book, of course.

"Oh, that was absolutely perfect," Everett said,

chuckling. "You switched keys and taunted the demon until it jumped into the vessel. Brilliant, Marcus, brilliant."

"I thought so," I said.

Everett glanced at Theo and said, "You must be Theo. Quick thinking about the copper wire, lad."

Theo stood with his mouth open. It was the first time I'd ever seen him speechless.

"Is that Michael Swenor's book?" Lu asked.

"Aye. And quite the story it is," Everett replied. "Turns out it wasn't just about delivering the Paradox key to you, Marcus. It was about recapturing the Boggin. That's the event that finally ended his tale."

Everett held the book out to us so we could read the final page. At the bottom, beneath the last paragraph, were two beautiful words.

" 'The end,' " I read aloud.

"My two favorite words," Everett said. "Now all it needs is a title. Every book has to have a title."

We all stood there, at a loss, until . . .

"What about *Mysterious Messenger*?" Theo said.

We all shot him a surprised look.

Theo shrugged and said, "You know, because Michael Swenor brought the key to Marcus. And all that."

"I don't know" I said. "There ended up being so much more to the story than that."

"Then let's just call it what it was," Lu said. *"Curse of the Boggin."*

Everett raised an eyebrow and looked to me.

"That's more like it," I said.

"Then *Curse of the Boggin* it is!" Everett declared as he snapped the book shut. "Welcome to the party, Theo."

Theo rubbed his ear and gave me a small smile.

Everett said, "Now I can place it with the other Boggin stories, in the *Completed* section."

We watched as Everett ambled to the aisle of completed stories and shelved the newest volume.

"What do I do with this?" I asked, pushing the vessel across the desk. "It's not like I can keep it in my room next to my football trophies."

"Bury the beastie," Everett said. "Stick it in a vault. Find a place where nobody will find it. What happened here wasn't the first time. I've got aisles of stories that say so."

"I guess I'll have to figure something out," I said.

"That's not all that needs figuring out," Everett said. "There's the issue of that missing book. We still don't know why Michael Swenor released the Boggin, or who put him up to it. There's a whole other story in play here."

"We saw my parents out on the water," I said. "My birth parents."

"They were, like . . . ghosts," Theo said.

Lu said, "Were they *like* ghosts . . . or were they ghosts?"

"Give me a break," Theo shot back. "I'm out of my comfort zone here."

"I think the missing book is my parents' story," I said. "It could be about what really happened to them."

"Does that mean you'll be trying to finish it?" Everett asked.

All eyes went to me.

I gazed down one of the long aisles of books that held the unfinished stories. It was daunting to see so many thousands of books, all containing stories of people from different times and places whose lives had been disrupted. As Everett said, there was no way to know what would happen with any of them, because it hadn't happened yet. But there was one thing we did know.

The stories could be finished.

"Not knowing who my real parents were and what happened to them has bothered me my whole life. The way I see it, I've got a shot at putting a few of my own ghosts to rest. While I'm at it, I might be able to help some of the other people who are locked in their own mysteries."

"Like me," Lu said.

"And me," Theo added.

I looked to Everett and said, "I've got two research projects for you."

"I'd be honored," Everett said with a wink. "It's what I do."

"You'll need help, Marcus," Lu said.

"Absolutely," Theo added. "From somebody smarter than you."

"Yeah," Lu said. "And from Theo too."

Theo shot her a withering look.

Lu just smiled.

"Seriously? You guys would help me tackle some of these mysteries?"

"Wait," Lu said. "You're asking if I'm willing to go on mysterious adventures filled with danger and excitement? Do you know me? Have we met?"

"That's a yes," Theo said.

I looked to Everett and said, "Then you've got yourself three new agents."

But before we could even think about tackling a new story, I had some other important business to settle.

On Sunday afternoon I sat in the park near the Stony Brook train station with Lillian Swenor. Alec was off playing on the swings. He didn't seem all that interested in seeing me. I figured it was because he was still upset about giving me the key. They were two people whose lives were never going to be the same, thanks to the curse of the Boggin. I needed to let Mrs. Swenor know that Michael was at peace, though I didn't think for a second she'd believe me. Still, I had to try. I sat there for the longest time, trying to find the right words.

As it turned out, she said them for me.

"Is Michael's story finished?" she asked.

I was so surprised by the question that I didn't know how to answer. She looked at me with a twinkle in her eye that gave me a hint of the bright personality she must have had before Michael died.

"Don't look so surprised," she said. "Michael told me a little about the Library. To be honest, I didn't believe him. I didn't want to believe. But I do now."

"Then, yes, his story is finished," I said. "I don't think I'm going to be seeing him anymore."

Mrs. Swenor sighed and said, "That's a good thing, I guess. Thank you, Marcus."

"For what?"

"Michael's at peace now, and so am I."

Alec came running over, out of breath from doing laps around the slide.

"Can we go now?" he asked his mother.

"Not yet," I said. "Alec, I'm sorry for taking the key. I know how much it meant to you because it was your dad's, and I feel bad that I had to take it."

Alec shrugged and looked to the ground without a word.

"But I think I can replace it with something way better," I said.

I reached into my hoodie pocket.

"My father wanted me to have that key," I said. "And I'm pretty sure your father would want you to have this."

I pulled out Michael Swenor's New York City firefighter's badge. Alec's eyes lit up as I held the treasure out to him in my open palm.

"Michael's first badge! I thought that was lost," Mrs. Swenor exclaimed. "Where did you find it?"

"It was being held by a good friend until it could get to where it belongs, and it belongs with you, Alec."

Alec looked to his mom for the okay. Mrs. Swenor nodded enthusiastically. Alec didn't wait another second and took the precious badge. His father's badge. He gazed at it as if it was the most valuable treasure he could imagine. Because it was.

"Thanks, Marcus," Alec said. "I wish you knew my dad. You would have liked him."

"I know I would have," I said.

Mrs. Swenor pinned the badge onto Alec's jacket.

Alec couldn't have been prouder, and neither could I. In that moment, any doubts I had were completely washed away. I wanted to do whatever I could to help the people whose lives were haunted by the unfinished stories of the Library. The opportunity to do that was a gift from my father, and I was ready to accept it.

A few days later, Theo, Lu, and I were back out on the water in Lu's father's speedboat.

I had gotten some copper pipe from Home Depot and talked the shop teacher at school into melting it down and sealing the seams of the vessel. I told him it was an art project. He didn't question me. I think he just liked to play with the furnace and pour molten metal.

My next stop was at a nautical-supply store, where I found the heaviest anchor chain I could load into my pack without it pulling me off my bike. I also bought a twenty-eight-pound navy anchor.

We checked some nautical charts online and found the deepest section of the Sound that was close enough to cruise to. It took only twenty minutes in Mr. Lu's crazy-fast boat to get to the spot.

It was a still, sunny day. Once Lu killed the engine, all was peaceful and silent. Nobody said it, but we were all scanning the horizon for fear the Boggin might still be able to conjure up a rogue storm.

There was nothing to see but a clear blue sky and fluffy white clouds.

The Boggin no longer had any power.

This was its funeral.

A burial at sea.

"Should we say a few words?" Theo asked as we stood together in the stern of the boat.

The vessel sat on the bench seat, wrapped in chains that were hooked to the anchor.

"Yeah, good riddance," Lu said.

"Part of me doesn't want to do this," I said.

"You can't be serious!" Theo exclaimed.

"I'm not. Not really. I hope this thing stays down there for a thousand years."

"How about forever?" Lu said.

"I know, but I can't help but feel like the truth about what happened to my parents is going to be trapped down there with it."

"Don't go there, Marcus," Lu cautioned. "Michael Swenor broke the seal, and look where that got him."

"That's another thing," I said. "If my father captured the Boggin twelve years ago, you have to believe he would have hidden the vessel where nobody would find it."

"Yeah, so?" Lu asked.

"So then how did Michael Swenor get it? Who was the guy that contacted him before he unsealed the vessel? And why did Swenor break the seal? What was he trying to do?"

The questions hung heavily as we stared at the chain-wrapped box.

"Maybe some mysteries are better off left a mystery," Theo said.

I didn't buy that for a second. That was one mystery I was determined to solve.

"Let's do this," I announced.

It took all three of us to lift the weighted-down container up onto the rail of the boat. We held it there, teetering on the edge. Lu took Theo's arm and gently pulled him away, leaving me holding the vessel on my own.

"All you, Marcus," she said.

I looked at the vessel and said, "I don't know if you can hear me, but I'm going to find the truth. I'm going to get that book, and I'm going to figure out what happened to my parents. And you know what else? That library you hate so much? We're going to finish a lot more of those stories, and there's nothing you can do about it. You may have all the time in the world, but you're going to spend it at the bottom of the ocean, wondering how you were outsmarted by a bunch of annoying children."

I gave the box a gentle nudge, and it fell over, splashing down hard onto the water. Theo and Lu quickly joined me, and we watched as the metallic package quickly disappeared into the darkness of the green water.

My gaze drifted up and out over the expanse of the Sound. It was another perfect fall day. There were no other boaters out except for one lone sailboat that glided along in the distance, headed for the sea. It wasn't close enough for me to know for sure, but I wanted to believe my birth parents were on board, maybe with Michael Swenor, enjoying another beautiful day out on the water.

"I'm going to finish your story," I said aloud. "I promise."

ABOUT THE AUTHOR

D. J. MacHale is the author of the bestselling book series Pendragon, the spooky Morpheus Road trilogy, and the sci-fi thriller trilogy The SYLO Chronicles. In addition to his published works, he has written, directed, and produced numerous award-winning television series and movies for young people, including *Are You Afraid of the Dark?*, *Flight 29 Down*, and *Tower of Terror*. D.J. lives with his family in Southern California. Visit him at djmachalebooks.com.